Bomb

Rook & Ronin Book Six

HᵃUSS

Edited by RJ Locksley
Cover Design by JA Huss

Dedication

For the ones we lost and found again…

JA HUSS

CHAPTER ONE

"Spencer! Fuck, dude! Watch the fucking road!" Ronin grabs the wheel and I tap the brake to stop for the light at College and Laurel.

"Ronin, was that Ronnie back there?" I'm trying my best to check the side view to see, but it's no use. The girl went into the restaurant. "I think that was Ronnie walking into Anna Ameci's."

"How unusual," Ford replies dryly from the back of the surveillance van, "for a woman to be going into a restaurant at dinnertime."

I check the rear view so I can talk shit to his image. "Well, that woman was with a man. A man who is not me, so uh, yeah, asshole, it's pretty fucking unusual for Ronnie to be having dinner with someone who is not me."

"Since when?" Ford asks as he types away on that stupid keyboard. "I see her out with men all the time."

"*What?*"

"Ford, goddammit, what'd I tell you?" Ronin interjects.

"You know about this?" I ask Ronin.

"She's not your girlfriend, Spencer. Rook says she's got a few other good prospects."

"A few other… what the fuck? Since when?"

"Since you ignore her and treat her like shit," Ford says, still tapping away.

A horn honks behind me and I look back to the road. The light is green so I move forward with the rest of traffic and then turn left on Elizabeth. "Eye on the prize, Spence," Ronin says from the passenger seat. "Just focus on what the hell we're doing. You can figure out what's going on with Ronnie later."

Yeah, easy for him to say. Fuckass. He's got Rook at home. And hell, even Ford has a fucking girl at home. And a baby for Christ's sake. And my best booty call is out on the town with another fucking guy!

"Turn left, turn left, Spencer!" Ronin yells. "Fuck."

"I was gonna turn left all along, calm down, Larue."

He shoots me a dirty look at the nickname but I don't give a shit. I love calling his whipped ass Larue.

"Spencer, you can go home if you want to act childish. Ronin and I can do this alone."

"Fuck off, Ford. Get your toy ready, we're almost there."

"I'm ready," he says, leaning up to the front cab. He's holding the little robot that looks a lot like a two-pound dumbbell with antennae. "Where's he now, Ronin?"

Ronin looks down at the tablet in his hand. "Same place. At the bar, just ordered another drink."

"So we have a little buffer then, right?" I ask. "He's gonna nurse that thing?"

"Dunno," Ronin says with a huff. "He's got a shot and a beer, which means it could just be a chaser. Better get it in quick, Ford. And I swear to God, Spencer, if we get busted for this stupid shit, I will have your ass."

"Stupid shit? This asshole stole seven fucking bikes out of my showroom! That's like eighty grand! It's not some stupid shit."

"Allegedly stole. You have no proof. And eighty grand is not worth the attention this close to the trials," Ford replies back. "But I'm clean on this."

4

Ronin laughs. "Ford, we're using a military-grade robot to spy on Spencer's competitor, you really think if we get caught we're clean? Please. We're the first people they'll pick up."

"Anyway… we're here. This close enough, Ford?" I pull up a few blocks down from the warehouse that Drake Cikes calls home base. "Cikes Bikes. What the fuck is that?" I ask, pointing up to the sign near the entrance to his part of the complex. "And he just has to open up shop in Fort Collins? You know what he's doing, don't you? Trying to confuse people. Cikes Bikes and Shrike Bikes sound the same, and if you look us up online, he comes up Fort Collins and I come up Bellvue. People think his stupid bikes are mine! He's getting my business and now he stole from me! Hell, I bet you anything he's chopped up those bikes and has my fucking parts on his custom shit right now!"

"Calm down, Spencer," Ronin says. "We don't know any of that yet. And there's no way anyone can mistake you for him, so just relax."

Well, that is true. Because I'm all tatted up in black and red. I've got the body of a Greek god, and I own this fucking town. Drake is one of those rockabilly types, with his skinny-ass body, thick black glasses, and white t-shirts. "Thinks he's Fonzie or something."

"What?" Ronin asks with a weird look.

"Drake. Thinks he's Fonzie with those white t-shirts. And him stealing my bikes is his version of jumping the shark. He's desperate, so he's gotta steal my shit."

"You're crazy, Spencer." Ronin goes back to his tablet.

"Crazy enough to come up with this plan, *yo*."

I might've gone too far became they're ignoring me now.

5

"OK," Ford says, "I'm gonna drop it." He opens the back door of the van and tosses the robot out. Ronin switches feeds so he has the bot cam on one side of his tablet and Ashleigh manning the Drake cam on the other. She's new in town and no one really knows her yet, so she was the only one who could keep an eye on the guy while we tapped his shit.

The bot's all-terrain tires start to roll and it travels down the alley to the warehouse. The bay door is closed. We've been watching this place all week and it's the same routine. Drake takes off about four-thirty and heads over to the Cat Call for dunch and a few brewskies. Then he comes back and locks the place up. We've looked at every possible way to get in here without resorting to the stealth and stalk we're doing now, but the place is tight. Ford even hacked the blueprints of the building from the city, and no dice. The place was remodeled before he moved in last month and it's like these guys are stashing guns and gold in there.

But Drake always pulls into the bay when he comes home, he likes to work on his bike in the evenings or something because he stays late every night. So the bay will open to let the bike in and that will be our window to drive that bot right into his lair, the mechanical hum of the tiny motor covered up by the roaring of the motorcycle.

He's got quite the setup for a man who came out of nowhere. Warehouse, employees, production schedule, advertising. It's like he's got a backer or something. But Ford checked him out. There are no obvious ties and no covert ones either. None Ford can see without taking risks that are not warranted for this particular annoyance.

At least as far as Ronin is concerned. And since Ronin's the one who has to dig us out if we fuck up, he always gets the final say on shit like that.

The radio in back crackles and then Ashleigh's voice comes in. "This is Mama Likes a Spankin', come back good, buddies."

I look at Ronin. He shakes his head. "You don't want to know," he says.

"Go ahead, Red Cheeks," Ford replies.

"Playtime's over, time to get busy. ETA"—her voice is drowned out by a loud motorcycle starting up and driving away—"five. Mama out."

"Someone's been watching a little too much *Dukes of Hazzard*."

Both my partners in crime ignore me now. Figures. I'm always the bored one on these jobs. I never have anything to do unless someone needs to be roughed up. And this guy can't be roughed up. He's too close to me. But that guy with Ronnie back at Anna Ameci's can.

I crack my knuckles and pat my leather jacket until I find the outline of my little Smith and Wesson Bodyguard. Love this little gun. It fits everywhere. In a pocket, in a boot—and shit, my hands are so big, I can probably conceal it in my palm. It's always there, inside left pocket of the leather, ready to go when I am.

A motorcycle roars by and the van shakes a little from the wind and the rumble.

We watch the bike on the bot cam, then it inches forward into the bay with the bike. "We're in. Now all I gotta do is find a place to park it."

"Find that place now, Ford. Else we're fucking busted." Ronin says with urgency.

I lean over and watch the feed as Ford tries to maneuver the bot under a tool bench. The little cam picks up the bike and Ford backs the bot up and does a neat little three-point turn until it's concealed. "One and done," he says. "Let's

7

go. I can come back later when the place is locked up to reposition."

He doesn't have to tell me twice. I start the van and pull out, taking the long way around the block, and then head up towards Mulberry. Ronin's truck is parked on Laurel, but I drop Ford off first. Ashleigh is waiting for him at the FoCo Cinema where Rook was watching their kid until her job was done. Rook's already walking down the road towards the prearranged meeting place for Ronin to pick her up.

After I ditch everyone I park the van in the alley behind Big City Burrito and head back up towards Anna Ameci's. I enter through the back door where the bathrooms are and sneak up towards the dining room. It's not a fancy place, just a family restaurant, but that sure the fuck is Veronica having dinner with a dude. And they are both dressed like they work on Wall Street.

I let out a long breath and wait it out, because the waiter just dropped off the check. They get up and the guy puts his hand at the small of her back, guiding her away from a large group who are jostling everyone near the door.

What a player. That's my move.

I can't see them after they go through the door, so I slip back out the way I came and walk the wall down the alley that takes me back out to College Ave.

I'm just rounding the corner when the guy slams into me. He backs off, apologizing, then keeps walking. I peek around the corner and catch Veronica getting into her little Mini Cooper parked in front of Sick Boyz Inc., the tattoo shop she runs with her father and brothers. I turn back to the scumbag trying to bag my girl and walk silently down the alley. He's looking at his phone, standing next to a dark-colored sedan. I slip the gun out of my pocket and walk up behind him and place it against his head.

"Do not move," I whisper.

He freezes and I pat him down until I find his wallet, and then slip it out. I want to ask him so many questions, but I can't. Not without risking my identity. I clock him on the head and he crumples against the car and then folds until he's on the ground. I take his ID and throw the wallet down as he moans and starts checking his head for damage. I walk off, calmly. He never comes after me, but even if he did, he wouldn't find me. I know this downtown well enough to make it back to the alley behind Big City Burrito without being on the street.

I don't loiter when I get to the van, just start it up and head back to the shop up in Bellvue.

Fuck, what a night. I palm the guy's ID and wonder what the hell he's doing with my Ronnie.

He's not her type, but she sure didn't look like my type tonight. Not in that tan skirt-suit and trench coat.

This throws me. Ronnie has never looked the part of tattoo artist. She's wild and she's got big hair and bigger boobs, but she has no tats. Not even one. She's got a severe blood aversion and I've always been surprised that she can put up with the little pinpricks of blood that bubble up when she's working. So maybe a businessman *is* her type.

I chew on this the whole ride back to Shrike Bikes, my thoughts as twisted and unsettled as the Poudre River that's raging with an early spring thaw right alongside the road. And when I get home and park the van in a locked building at the back of the property, I come to the conclusion that Ronnie's type just might be a businessman after all.

But I'm a businessman too. I might not look like one, but I am *all* fucking business.

And if she wants to play a game to see if I'm serious, well, I can play as well as anyone.

In fact, I'm a damn good player.

I'm the best fucking player this town has ever seen.

So game on.

CHAPTER TWO

I jingle my keys in my hand as I walk back up to the house. I pass by the shop and sigh. We're moving into town for Shrike Bikes Season Two. Biker Channel has had about enough of Bellvue—too fucking small. And really, this isn't even Bellvue. I live ten miles north of the intersection that thinks it's a town.

But I like it out here. It's quiet. Too quiet for some, but not for me. I spent a lot of time here growing up because this was my gran's house. So it's always felt like home.

I brokered a deal with the Biker Channel people though, got them to foot the cost of renovation of the new shop if I bought the building. They do get to put a bunch of promo material in the shop, which is fine, I guess. The more people watching the Biker Channel, the more people watching the Shrike Bikes show. That's more money for me. Win-win.

Last fall Rook was annihilated in the media when she took her story public and outed a huge human trafficking ring in Chicago. She got a lot of publicity for the show because she's been part of this project since the beginning. First as my body art model for the Sturgis pilot show, then as the Shrike Bikes receptionist for Season One. But no one knew that Season One would be almost all about her. No one knew all that shit would go down and change the whole production schedule. But the publicity worked in my favor and I renegotiated the contract with the Biker Channel to get the building remodel paid for.

I key in the security code to the house and let myself in the kitchen, throw my keys down on the granite counter top, and open the fridge. Empty.

I haven't eaten at home in a while. We've just been too busy in town getting ready for the new season. In fact, I haven't even built a bike in over a month. I slam the fridge door closed and open the pantry.

Mac and cheese. And Campbell's Soup. I'm living like a fourteen-year-old who has no parents.

Fuck. I take the businessman's ID out of my pocket and study it. He's got his hair slicked back, and not in that *I'm dangerous* way like Ford does it. No. This guy's hair says *I use product*. In fact, this asshole's hair says *I have a stylist*. Not a barber, a stylist. I bet he gets his fingers done while he's there. And his toes.

Asshole.

I'm on fucking TV and I don't even let the makeup girls touch my fucking hair. I just buzz that shit off when it gets too long.

I check him out again. Banker. I bet he's a fucking banker. He looks like one. Wearing some fancy suit like he's important. Plus, he's got beady eyes. Beady brown eyes, says his ID. That's a sure sign that he's no good. Every cartoon connoisseur knows that beady eyes are a tell.

I study him for a few more seconds. He's even got a suit on in his driver's license photo. I glance over to his name. Carson. What kind of stupid name is Carson?

Last name of Reed—Veronica Reed? Nope. Ronnie Reed? Fuck, that one sounds pretty good. But Veronica Vaughn has always hated the fact that her names start with the same letter.

I happen to like it, myself. And my name is the shit. Spencer Shrike. It's got a nice ring to it.

Veronica Shrike? Maybe.

Ronnie Shrike. Better.

Ron the Bomb Shrike? I laugh at that. Fucking girl makes me smile even when she's not here. I sigh. Fucking Ronnie. I fish my phone out of my pocket and flop down on the couch. I press her number in my contacts and wait as the phone rings.

Voicemail. *"You've reached Ronnie Vaughn. I'm either working or playing. If you need me for either, leave a message and I'll get back to you!"* She makes a slurpy kissing sound and then the beep.

"Hey, Ronnie. You should come over. Call me back." I sigh again and pocket my phone, but it buzzes an incoming call before I can release it, so I pull it back out. I look at the screen. "Yello, baby! Wanna come over?"

"Oh," she says. "It's you. I was expecting a call from the bank. I deleted your number and didn't recognize it, sorry."

"What? You deleted my number? For why?" I'm stunned. Like my hand is up in the air and I'm mid-shrug with wide eyes.

"Why? *Why?* You have some fucking nerve, Spencer. I haven't talked to you since fucking Halloween!"

13

She's on drugs. She might need a blood test. "I took you out for New Year's, you hot little amnesiac."

"No, you did not take me *out*. You *saw me* at Antoine's. Dates pick up their girlfriends, Spencer."

"We ate, we drank, we fucked. How is that not a date?" This is what dates usually entail.

She growls at me though the phone. "The food was free, the drinks were free, and I was too drunk to remember most of the fuck, so it hardly counts. I definitely don't recall an orgasm."

"Ha!" I pull the phone away from my ear and find the voice memos, then push play on the one dated New Year's.

"*Ohhhh, Spencer!*" Veronica wails in the recording. "*Baby, yes!*"

My phone does the three-beep thing that says the call ended. I laugh and call her back. It rings through again. "Ronnie, come on! It was funny, you know it was. Since when does this shit piss you off?" I stop talking. And wait. I'm not sure why, it's a fucking voicemail, she's not gonna respond. I frown and let out a sigh. "Well, fuck. You're mad, I guess. Sorry, Rons. Seriously. Call me back, OK?"

I end the call and slump back against the couch. It hasn't been that long since I saw her, has it? I know we were pretty drunk on New Year's but I spent the night with her down in Rook's old garden apartment. What more does she want? She knows I'm busy and I've got shit going on. I can't have her hanging around too much or people will think we're together.

I can't have people thinking we're together.

My phone buzzes in my hand again and I look at the screen with some hope. "Arrrgh. Fucking Ford." I press his ugly mug to answer the call. "Yeah?"

"Meet me tonight at midnight so we can take the van back over to Fonzie's and reposition."

"I don't wanna go out at midnight. Can't you just do it?"

"Spencer," Ford says in that new parenting voice he has. "You're worse than Kate. You're the driver in this scheme, so drop your balls and do your job. Pick me up at my place at midnight."

I get triple beeps again.

"God!" I slam my fist down on the coffee table. I'm just the guy everyone gets to shit on tonight. And I'm starving. I pocket Carson's ID and get back up, grab my keys, and head outside to my Shrike Bikes truck. Might as well go into town and get something to eat. Then I can stop by Ronnie's and sweeten her up with some love. She's so damn excitable. She's always been like that, from the first moment I saw her.

Not met her. *Saw* her. Because I saw her weeks before I finally made my move.

I had just started up fall semester at Colorado State after transferring from University of Denver to get away from Ronin senior year. This was after all that shit went down with Mardee and the Boulder asshole ended up dead. Our team was in desperate need of a break. And I was walking by the CSU bookstore heading into Engineering for my mandatory science class, and there she was.

Throwing a fit.

"Who the hell died and made you king?" the bombshell blonde screams at a huge mother all tatted up with dragons down his arms. She pushes him in the chest, straining to make the mountain of a man move. He folds his arms and yawns.

15

I figure this is her boyfriend so I stop dead in my tracks to see if the guy makes a move to hit her back. She's irate, he's calm. No one's paying any attention to them whatsoever. In fact, even though it's between classes and there are probably more than a hundred people walking the path with me, these two have a nice big circle of space around them.

And being the smart motherfucker that I am, I deduce that's because these two have a reputation.

So I cop a seat on a cement planter and pull out a smoke. She pushes him at least a half dozen more times, she yells at him. Some professor comes over and tries to intervene and the bombshell whirls around so fast the poor nerd has to step back from her fury.

The campus police show up after that and break it up, but then Bomb and Tat guy walk away—together, how ridiculous is that after all her stomping—and I notice they have the same logo on the backs of their shirts.

Sick Boyz Inc.

A tattoo shop on College in downtown Fort Collins.

I had one tattoo back then. And it was fucked up. I told Bobby Choo down at Choo's Tattoos in Capitol Hill in Denver I wanted a raven on my back. He gave me a hula girl.

I beat the everliving shit out of Bobby Choo. I tattooed his eyes up black and blue.

Hey, I rhymed.

So I was looking for an artist and I figured that if this bombshell worked at Sick Boyz, I needed to check that out because I could certainly enjoy her hands all over my back a helluva lot more than fucking Bobby Black and Blue Eyes. I stalked her good. I'm an accomplished stalker. Recon is part of my team job. Ford does the virtual things, but I'm the guy on the ground.

So I reconned Bombshell. She was an art major, senior year like me. She had four brothers, all of whom worked at Sick Boyz, and she had just started out there as well. I learned that from the website. They have a bio on all the artists online and a fifty-year history of the shop from the time her gramps started it in the sixties.

And the website gave me another vital piece of information. That guy she was yelling at was her *brother*.

Game on.

I liked the Bombshell immediately. Her hair was long, so blonde it was almost golden, and her eyes were big and blue. She did wear a lot of make-up, but I'm not one of those guys who thinks that's a bad thing. I like fuck-me eyes and her lips could be green for all I cared back then. And the Spencer Shrike of today knows damn well those lips are magical.

And from the second I walked into Sick Boyz to check her out in person, I knew.

I wanted her. Bad.

CHAPTER THREE

Sick Boys Inc., Three years ago

The Stray Cats blares out of hidden speakers as I push through the entrance to Sick Boyz and the sounds of downtown Fort Collins are muffled once the door swings closed behind me. Bombshell is at the register, ringing up some guy who has a small square of red-speckled white gauze covering the top of his left wrist. He's got full sleeves, so this is acceptable in my opinion. The wrist is not something you do alone if you're a guy.

The guy pays, tips, flirts, and leaves as I peruse the art on the wall. There's a lot of pictures of Bombshell in here too. Starting with her in bouncy blonde pigtails looking to be about six. I laugh a little just as the music is turned off.

"Something funny?" Bombshell asks from behind the register.

I turn and watch her shuffle though the day's receipts. It's late, just about closing time, so I'm not here for a tattoo. I'm here for a date. Otherwise known as an appointment.

"This you in the picture?" I ask, using my polite Catholic-school manners.

"Yeah," she replies, not looking up at me. "That's me. All twenty-seven pictures of the little blonde girl on that wall are me. Can I help you with something? I'm just about to lock up."

I walk over to her and lean down on the glass counter, checking out the aftercare products they have for sale. "I've got some fucked-up work I need fixed." I stand up straight and look down at her. She's not short—average height, really. Maybe five six or seven. But I'm tall, so I tower over her. She looks up at me and this makes her big blues look even bigger. God, this girl is like a pin-up from the good ol' days. Her tits are like melons. Big, round melons that are practically begging for my giant hands to manhandle them.

"Eyes up, perv," she says dryly as she traces a line from her cleavage to her chin. "I'm up here, big boy."

I grab the hem of my t-shirt and slowly drag it up my body, exposing my chest, then pull it forward over my head.

Her eyes are plastered to my abs. Actually, I'm pretty sure they're darting back and forth between the v line and the happy trail.

"Hey, Bombshell," I say. She swallows and looks up at me. "You can look at me all night long. Fuck me with your eyes for all I care."

She recoils a little, like I might've insulted her. But surely a girl who is not only a tattoo artist in a college town, but also grew up with four brothers, could not be that easily offended.

"Watch your mouth, asshole. Or I'll stuff my fist through your teeth," she snarls.

Or maybe she is. I hold my hands up in an *I surrender* gesture and turn around so she can see my back.

"What the fuck is that?" She snickers down a laugh and I roll my eyes and sigh.

"A mistake, hence the need for a fix. Can you make anything out of this?" I jolt a little when her fingers touch my left shoulder blade, and then trace down what I think is the hula girl's leg.

"God, I've never seen an uglier tattoo."

I look over my shoulder at her, kinda irritated. "Can you fucking fix it or not?"

She smirks at me and then traces it again, making me shudder. "I can," she whispers, and then clears her throat. "But my brother Vic is probably your best bet."

I turn around and her fingertips drag along my arm and stop on my chest. "What if I don't want your brother to do it? What if I came in here specifically to get you to do it?"

She stares up at me, her chest heaving a little, making her tits expand. As if that was even necessary. Her tits are spectacularly large. She blinks at me a few times, like she's coming to some kind of realization. Like she's deciding I might be hot.

"My brothers will beat the shit out of you if you think you can come in here and flirt your way into an appointment with me. I'm not on the books for new appointments. I only see regulars. So, if you'd like me to set up a consult with Vic, I'll be more than happy to do that for you. Otherwise, get the hell out of the shop. It's eleven o'clock and we're closed."

"Well…" I stretch my neck a little as I lean over the glass case, clasp my hands together, and get comfortable. "I can see I'm gonna have to unleash the charm on you."

Her hand is a blur of motion and the next thing I know, the blunt end of a pink .38 Special is pressed up against my skin. And yeah, she's got a gun against my head but the only thing I can think about is how her tits are being squished against the glass in front of me as she leans over.

"Fuck, Bombshell, that is the hottest shit I've ever seen." And it is. I'm hard right now as I play that move back in my head. I laugh.

"It's not hot or funny," she growls at me. "I'm dead serious. Get the fuck out of the shop."

I grab her wrist and twist until she drops the gun. It clatters to the ground as I pull her over the case, swing her over my shoulder, and then twirl her around and set her ass back down on the glass. I hold her wrists for a few seconds and then step back and take in her reaction.

She screams.

I slap my hand over her mouth and laugh. "Shit! Stop already. I'm not gonna hurt ya, Bomb, I'm playing." Her muffled screams have made my palm moist and this is weirdly erotic to me.

She stops screaming and just stares at me.

"You OK?"

She nods her head.

"I can remove the gag order and you'll be calm?"

She shrugs.

"I'll take that as a yes." I remove my hand and she stays quiet, so I lean down to pick up the little pink gun and get the feel of it. "Now, you care to explain to me why you're pulling out a gun that's not loaded?"

"It's loaded," she retorts, scowling.

"Nah," I say back as I twirl the little pink gun on my finger. "I know what a loaded .38 Special feels like, and this isn't it, sweetheart. If you're gonna threaten someone with a gun, might as well keep the bullets where they belong." I offer her the gun but as soon as reaches for it, I pull it back. "Let's make a deal, how about that?"

She snatches the gun away from me and scoffs. "You're in no position to make any deals, buddy. My brothers are gonna kick your ass."

I smile and study her intently. "Is that right? Because the way I see it, all I gotta do is tell them how easily you were overtaken tonight and your ass will be banned from any alone time at the shop for good." She gasps and looks shocked. "So let's make a deal and you can get some shop-time freedom and I can get your talented hands on my back, fixing that ugly-ass tattoo."

Her hands come up at the same time and she shoves me hard on the shoulders, trying to get me to back up and give her space. I don't even move an inch. Instead, I grab each of her knees and open up her legs so I can slide right between them.

"Back off!" she growls.

I press my palms on either side of her faded-jean-covered thighs and lean in until we're face to face, her blue eyes looking up at me in surprise. "No. I want an appointment with you. Give me one."

She kicks out and struggles, then tries to scoot back across the glass and escape that way, but I grab her calves and slip my hands behind her knees and squeeze until she squirms, stifling down a tickle laugh.

"Don't," she says through her squealing. "Stop it!" She laughs.

I ease up so she can stop wiggling against my grip. "Give me what I want, Bombshell. And I'll walk out of here and I won't come back until our date."

"Date?" she scoffs. "An appointment is not a date. There's no fucking way I'm dating an asshole like you. You

23

think you can come in here, manhandle me, threaten me, and get—"

I kiss her. I crush her mouth silent, slip in my tongue, slide my hands up to her tits, squeeze hard enough to make her moan, and then grab her hair and keep her there.

She kisses me back, her pouty red lips pressing against mine. She's panting hard as I pull us apart and she actually moans.

Fuck yeah.

"I want a tattoo appointment, Veronica Vaughn. Give me a date and a time, right the fuck now."

"Tomorrow at four," she breathes, her spectacular chest once again heaving.

I shoot her with my finger and wink. "I'll see you then, Bombshell. Be ready for me." And then I turn and walk away.

"Wait!" she calls. "What's your name? And how do you know *my* name?"

I don't turn, just open the door and call out, "You'll know my name soon enough. And the rest is recon, baby. It's my job to know."

CHAPTER FOUR

I chuckle to myself as I live that memory over again in my mind. I had her. Man, I so, *so* had her the minute I walked into that place. She was feisty with her little pink .38 Special, but my lips are irresistible. They call to her, they suck her in places she's never dreamed of, they whisper dirty things in her ear and make her blush, tremble, and come all at the same time.

But her lips. Fuck. My bombshell's lips make me explode every single time. She's got a pucker that won't quit. She's got a tongue that can swirl a pattern in my mouth so erotic, I just want to throw her down on the ground and fuck the life out of her. She uses her teeth with such skill, it makes me hard just thinking about them. And when you combine all of those things with the wetness of her mouth and the heat of her breath…

Fuck. I need her right now. Why the hell did I leave her alone so long? The commotion leftover from the human trafficking shit in Chicago died down months ago. Veronica was not pestered once during the whole debacle, I made sure of it. She's right about New Year's. She was pretty fucked up, but we still had a good time. We always have a good time, I just need to remind her how good it gets.

I press on the accelerator of the Shrike truck and speed towards Highway 14 that will take me into FoCo, then ease on into downtown and strain my neck looking down the street to see if her Mini Cooper is outside Sick Boyz. I hold out hope until I've passed it. That damn deathtrap always hides out among the trucks everyone else drives around here.

But no. I see her oldest brother Vic's bike, her father Vern's bike, her twin middle brothers Vinn and Vonn's bikes, and her baby brother Vann's Vespa.

I laugh at that. Poor Vann. The Vaughns are ruled by traditions. Everything they do has precedent. And in that family you cannot get a motorcycle until you build it yourself. Vann is only seventeen, and tradition also says you can't build your bike until you're eighteen. So the dirty, primer-covered classic Vespa is all he's allowed.

Sick Boyz must be going off tonight if the entire family is working at the same time, so it's interesting that Veronica isn't there to help. I swing a right on Mountain and head over to her house. She still lives at home. I pull up along their old brick monstrosity and scowl to myself. No Mini Cooper.

Gramps opens the door and waves at me to come inside.

Fuck. You don't say no to Gramps. He might be nine hundred years old, but he's got a mean streak. A sneaky mean streak. I park the truck in front, get out, and walk up to the open door. "Yo, Gramps! I'm looking for Ronnie, ya seen her?"

He comes out of the kitchen wearing a red-checkered apron around his waist, no shirt on, and flashing his five-hundred-year-old tattoos.

"Ahhhh, put some clothes on, ya old fart! No one wants to see your saggy shit."

He holds up a spoonful of pasta sauce and shoves it to my mouth. "Taste," he demands.

I slurp it and nod. "Yeah, it's good. It's always good. Tastes the same as last time. Ya seen Ronnie? I'm looking for her."

"At work," he barks as he goes back into the kitchen.

"No," I call out, walking after him. "I went by there, her car's not there."

"She walks now. Gonna sell it, so she parks it and walks."

"What?" She loves that car. "Since when? I just saw her in it like two hours ago." Gramps is busy stirring the pot on the stove. The whole place smells like an Italian restaurant. "Gramps," I try again. "Why does she want to sell her car?"

He looks over his shoulder. "I'm not allowed to tell you."

"What? Why the fuck not?"

"I'm not allowed to tell you that either. Go ask her, she's at the shop. And tell that son of mine to bring me some smokes on his way home."

"You quit smoking forty years ago, Gramps."

"Not for me, I have a date tonight, dumbass. Who you think I'm cooking for?"

I let out a long breath and feel a little sorry for myself as I walk out and get back in my truck. Ronnie's got secrets. Lots of them. She's having dinner with guys who are not me, she's selling her car, and she's slapped a gag order on Gramps.

This is adding up to something.

I swing the truck back out, flip a bitch, and head towards College Ave. I'm not sure what's going on with Ronnie, but I'm about to find out. I park next to Vann's gray primer-coated Vespa and head into the tattoo shop. I swing the door open and I'm accosted by frat boys all waiting around like idiots and looking at the sample art on the walls. That's one bad thing about living in a college town. College kids.

Of course, when Ronnie and I were in school together, we were the shit. But now that school is a distant memory best left forgotten, these kids annoy the fuck out of me. I've always lived out in Bellvue, even when I went to Colorado State for senior year, so I never had to put up with them much. But the new shop the Biker Channel and I decided on for Season Two is located a couple blocks up. Unlike my shop at home, this new shop will also have a showroom. So I expect the college kids will be dropping by often.

"Well, if it isn't Shrike fucking Bikes!" Vic's loud welcome blasts over the roar of excited frat boys and everyone turns to look at me.

"Where's Ron?"

Vic smiles that big-brother smile and that can only mean one thing. "She's not interested in talking to you, Shrike. Told me to tell you that if you came by."

I flip him off and walk down the hallway. Vic is not going to mess with me unless I ask for it. And a friendly *fuck you* is not enough to get us brawling. Because we've been down that road before. Once we start, we don't stop and there's always medical bills involved.

I look into each of the tat rooms as I pass. Vern's room is first, then Vic's, which is empty now since he's up front, then Vinn and Vonn—they share the biggest room—and finally Ronnie's room is last.

Her gun is buzzing, so I know she's got a customer. Her back is to the door so I slip in and lean over her shoulder. The customer is some wimpy eighteen-year-old, obviously a brother from the frat house since he's getting Greek letters on his non-existent bicep. "Beautiful, Ron. Love it, babe."

She never even flinches. Her machine never slows. She draws and wipes, and then draws again. Like I never said a word and I'm nobody.

I point to the other wimpy frat boy sitting in the only chair in the room. "Get the fuck out." He gets, and I sit, rolling my eyes as the plastic covering over the seat of the chair crinkles under my ass. Ronnie never even huffs. Usually that's what she does if I come in to her work acting like a caveman, but tonight I get nothing.

She's pissed.

I bide my time until she's done. She leaves and I stay put. I can hear her talking out in the lobby, then she tells her next victim to wait until she cleans the room and she'll be right back for him.

Ronnie is a freak about blood splatter from the tattoo machines. She wears scrubs to work. She has both a facemask and a visor with a clear plastic shield that covers her face. She wears gloves from the minute she walks into the shop until the minute she leaves and there's an air ionizer in the corner to clear out any microscopic bacterial byproducts that may or may not be floating around in the air.

Everything in this room is covered in plastic. From the tattoo chair to the cord on her tattoo machine. Even the flat screen mounted on the wall is covered in sheeting.

You really have to use your imagination when you watch TV in Ron the Bomb's room.

It takes her a good thirty minutes to remove all the plastic and apply new between customers. We've all learned to love this about her, even if she's constantly behind schedule.

She returns to the room crumpling her mask up and holding her face shield in her hand. "Why are you here?" she snaps at me.

I shrug. "I want to see you tonight."

She busts out a long low laugh as she shakes her head and starts pulling plastic off things. "Well, that's not going to happen, Spencer. I've got a date after work."

"I know," I say back calmly.

She looks over at me now, her eyebrows all scrunched up in confusion. "How do you know?"

"Because," I say sweetly, "your date's with me."

She whispers under her breath as she turns back to her room duties. "I'm busy, Spencer. Go away. Vic!" she yells over the music and buzzing of tattoo machines.

"Veronica," Vic says in his *how-can-I-help-you* voice. He must've been right outside the door. Asshole. "You need me to give him the boot?" Vic says with a smile in my direction.

"Please," she sighs. "I'm busy, Spencer. Just go away."

"Out, Spencer," Vic says. "She's working until eleven."

"Vic!" Ronnie screams. "What the fuck?"

Vic motions for me to follow him so I get up and grab Ronnie by the waist and haul her sexy little body up against mine. "Veronica Vaughn. You're mine tonight, baby. I'll be back at eleven. And don't think you can duck out early, because I've got my recon hat on right now. I've got a lot of questions for you and I'm just gonna spend the next few hours between now and then trying to answer them myself." I kiss her on the head and pat her ass gently as I leave.

I can hear her stomping her foot and growling out obscenities after I leave. Vic is waiting for me at the front door. He opens it and I walk through, then he follows.

"What's up?" I ask as I walk to my truck.

"You ever meet that new guy in town, Spencer? Drake what-the-fuck's-his-name?"

"Cikes," I hiss. "Drake Cikes. Is she going out with that fuck tonight?" Fucking Drake, I'll kill that mother—

"No, she's been sorta seeing an accountant or something. Real boring guy, she's into the boring ones right now."

"What?" She really is dating that fuck from the alley. "Wait, the boring *ones*? She's dating more than one?"

"Spencer, that's her business. I'm asking about that Drake fuck. Because I saw him over by your new place the other night. Stalking around the building. I was walking home from a fun night out with that redhead from Cat Call, and he was nosing around. And I know your showroom in Broomfield was just robbed. So—you know. He might be your guy."

I grunt a little but I don't give anything away. My team is in too deep with this shit to be copping out to some bullshit spouted off by Vic Vaughn. "Nah," I say. "I got a lead on that other incident, and it's not him."

Vic nods. I'm not sure if it's a conspiratorial nod or just a regular nod, so I let it go. "OK then. Take it easy. And Spencer?" I'm already turning to go when he calls me back. "Stay the fuck away from Veronica until she says otherwise. I will kick your ass over this. She's happy. I'm not sure what she's doing, but whatever it is, she's happy. Leave her alone."

And then he turns and walks back into the shop.

CHAPTER FIVE

Leave her alone, my ass.

I repeat that in my head over and over again as I wait for the girl at Big City Burrito to make my dinner. Fucking whatever. Ronnie is mine. Ronnie has always been mine. I own her ass. She's belonged to me since that very first night at the shop. And if she thinks I'm just gonna give her up after all these years, she's on some pretty powerful drugs.

I won't.

I might ignore her, but I have my reasons and that life is almost wrapped up. I can feel it. We're gonna wrap all that illegal shit up and move on. Ford's fucking married and has a kid, Ronin will have Rook roped in very soon, I can already see that shit coming. And I'll be damned if those two assholes think they're gonna become all mature and shit before I do.

Fuck that.

I'm the mature one on this team. I'm the one who has a real career. I've got three businesses, plus that little campground out in Nebraska. I'm on TV, I have my own line of custom bikes, and I've got the whole body art painting thing going. I'm bona fide. I'm on my way up. I've got plans, I've got big, big plans.

And Ron the Bomb has always been part of it. Shit, has that woman no memory? How could she have forgotten our first date?

"Shrike!" the burrito girl yells as she hands my dinner to Carla, the girl who runs the register.

I walk up to the counter and grab the bag. "*Gracias*, Carla."

"See ya *mañana*, Spencer."

She winks at me and I wink back and shoot her with my finger. "Tomorrow, baby. We're on. Pick you up at eight."

"I'll have my boots on, handsome!"

I chuckle as I walk out. Fucking Carla, gotta love that girl. She makes all my Thursday nights better. We've had a Thursday night date for almost two months now. I kinda like it too. She's one helluva cowgirl. Fridays I hang out with Renee from the Cat Call while she's at work. I got a new regular for Saturday. Kim from the Harley store down south in Broomfield. I don't usually go in there since I own my own bike shop and we sell or make everything I need custom. But I was looking for a specific set of pegs for the new bike I'm thinking about building, and I found a guy from Craigslist who had them, and he just happened to work at the Harley shop.

Sunday I go home to see the folks for dinner. It's a thing I can't get out of even if I wanted to. My old man would kick my ass if I didn't show up for family shit on Sundays.

So yeah, I haven't had much time for Ronnie, but I'm a busy fucking guy. What does she want me to do? Change my whole life around? I will, eventually, but not yet. I'm not ready for that yet. Too much shit to get done.

I get back in my truck and head home. Once I get past the little town of La Porte there's nothing else around, so I grab my burrito and start chowing. When you live thirty minutes away from the nearest real town, you learn to eat your take-out on the road. By the time I get home and let myself into the kitchen, my food is gone, my mood is even more sour, and I'm totally unsatisfied. I will go see Ronnie at eleven when she gets off, I do not care what Vic says. Ronnie and I have history.

I walk down the hallway towards my office and key in the code that controls the locks. This was Ronin's brilliant idea. And it *is* pretty brilliant. Key codes instead of keys. You always have a key and you always have a record of when the door is accessed.

I flip the light on and take it all in. Every wall is covered with pictures of Veronica. She was my body painting model for almost three years. I have touched every inch of her beautiful body with my paintbrush. And I do mean every inch. I even painted her hair once. She hated that and I laugh just thinking about it.

Our life together started the moment I saw her and Vic arguing outside the CSU bookstore. And while I did have to wrangle a gun out of her hand to get the first real date, the second time I talked to her, things went a whole other way.

JA HUSS

Colorado State University - Three years ago

"Miss Vaughn," I say sweetly as I saunter up to her. She's walking fast because she's late for her early morning art class.

"Go away, you caveman. I'll fix your stupid tattoo, but I'm not going to be nice about it. You kissed me, you know. Without permission."

"You liked it last night."

"Yeah, well, I was tired. And caught off guard. And manhandled." She quickens her pace to try and give me a hint, but I don't take hints. Besides, my legs are longer than hers. She can't out-power walk me.

"You liked all of that last night if I remember correctly."

She pulls open the door to the art building and I follow her in. We weave through the various displays in the shadowed room. "I like the art building," I tell her casually. Like we're just friends walking to class. "It's dark and moody. Like the artists who study here."

"Why are you following me?" she stops and asks in a huff, her foot stomping on the polished concrete floors.

"I'm going to class. I'm not following you."

She looks over at me and scowls. "You have class here in this building at seven AM? Not likely. There's only one class in here and it's by invitation only," she says with an air of superiority as she begins walking again.

I walk again too, then smile at her when she checks to see if I'm still following. "I've been invited, don't worry."

This makes her stop and whirl around to face me. "You're in my class?"

36

"I am," I say smugly. "I'm a transfer from DU. I major in business, but I take art on the side."

"Oh." She flips her long golden tresses over her shoulder. "A hobbyist."

"Yeah." I smirk and shrug at the same time. "You could call me that."

She turns again and resumes the power walk. I catch up, pass her, and then hold the studio door open and wave her through.

"Thank you," she says under her breath as she passes close enough for me to breathe in her scent. She smells like sugar. Seriously, like a fucking cookie or something. I watch her head across the room to gather her things. The studio is filled with students. At least forty of them. Everyone is setting up, getting ready for life drawing.

"Mr. Shrike," the middle-aged voice calls out to me from across the room.

I look over at Bombshell and she's watching me very carefully. I wink and shoot her with my finger, then turn and walk towards the professor with a smile. "Miss Aberdeen, thank you for fitting me in the class. I can see what you mean now, it's packed full."

She blushes at me. Yeah, I have that effect on women of all ages, so I shoot her a winning smile and tilt my head a bit. Ronin taught me that move. I might not be on speaking terms with him these days, but that guy knows all the fucking charm tricks. He has the women lined up like groupies.

I'm not a groupie gatherer, but this head-tilt thing works well enough on the professor in front of me. Her look says, *I'm an artist*. She's got the earthy clothes that hang off her skinny frame, the glasses, the put-up hair that's falling out all over the place, and the Birks on her feet.

She's so earthy, I was sorta shocked when she named her condition for letting me join this class.

"Mr. Shrike—"

"Please, Miss Aberdeen, call me Spence." I smile again and chance a look over at Bombshell. She's set up in the front row. I already knew this. I've been doing recon on the Bomb since I first saw her in that fight with her brother in front of the bookstore.

"Very well, Spence." Aberdeen blushes when she says my name and that's sorta cute. "Next week your space is next to Miss Vaughn—"

She continues talking about what will happen next week. But I'm more concerned with what's happening this week to give a shit about a time so far in the future, so I tune the rest out. I'm too busy looking over at the Blonde Bomb as she tries to process what's being said.

I chuckle as Aberdeen walks away and Veronica Vaughn walks up. "You planned this. You're stalking me, aren't you?"

"Recon, baby. Not stalking." And then I grab the hem of my shirt and pull it straight up over my head. Not too fast, Ronin taught me this too. He said the slow-mo shirt removal was one of the easiest ways to snag a girl. When I look back at Veronica her mouth is gaping open.

"What are you doing?" she hisses at me. "Put your shirt on!"

I drop the shirt to the floor and go for the pants. Veronica gasps when I pop the button and downright chokes when I go for the zipper. I hear a few cat calls from the back of the room as I slip my pants down.

I'm commando today, so His Highness just pops right out.

Every girl in the room explodes in laughter. It's the good kind though. I know the difference. This laughter says, *Holy fucking shit, I cannot believe he just took off his clothes!*

"You look more like a cherry than a bombshell right now, Blondie," I joke with her.

She shakes herself out of her silent stare and turns on her heel.

"Well," Miss Aberdeen says as she claps her hands together in delight. "Mr. Shrike—err, Spence." She smiles big as she says my name. "It's too late now, obviously, but next time—"

"Next time?" Blondie says as she peeks out from behind her easel.

"—please use the dressing room over there in the corner. And put on a robe until we're ready for you." She bats her eyelashes at me, then steals a glance down.

"Sure thing," I say as I wink and shoot. "Where do you want me, Miss Aberdeen?"

Veronica blushes the entire fucking class. Her face is this sexy shade of flush for ninety minutes. And every one of those ninety minutes, she thinks about nothing but me. She traces every line and curve of my body onto the paper in front of her. She licks her lips seventeen times. She sighs twenty-two times. She groans and whimpers when she makes five mistakes, and she even has a pouty frown on her face for the splittest of seconds when Aberdeen announces that class is over.

I wait for her as she cleans up. I'm wearing clothes again and all the girls, and a few dudes as well, are coming over to introduce themselves and ask who I am and where I came from.

I have that effect on people. I'm blessed in the body department. Ronin has his charm, Ford has his brain and I've got this beautiful body. *Plus* charm and brains. I'm the total package. Almost six foot three—I'm taller than both Ronin and Ford, and that's all muscle. I played a little football in high school and got two scholarship offers. But I stayed in town with Ronin and we both went to University of Denver.

The team comes before everything else—and DU is a great school anyway.

Ford was already in Boulder studying film, he's two years older. So Ronin and I started college together. He continued to model with Antoine, his sister's lover who runs Chaput Studios out of a remodeled six-story building near Lower Downtown. I continued to build bikes and learn how to run the business so I could take over Shrike Bikes from my old man. My mom was desperate to get him to retire after a heart attack a few years ago.

We roped Mardee into doing some cons with us. Some basic shit. Little bit of hands-on stealing from scumbags. Then she overdosed on heroin and died.

We didn't take it well, it was a huge blame game. Ford blamed Ronin, Ronin blamed me, I blamed—fuck. I blamed all of us. We were all at fault. We took it out on the local drug dealers using every skill we had in our arsenal. Namely Ford's savant hacking abilities. And all that ended abruptly after the Boulder job. The job that would change our lives, send me to Colorado State in Fort Collins and Ronin to University of Colorado in Boulder after we were kicked out of DU.

Of course, DU never said we were kicked out. But there's no way an institution of that caliber would allow us to stay. We saw the writing on the wall and Ronin and I don't come from the big shots around town. We have money, but not that kind of money. Not Ford money. We can't just donate enough money to purchase entire academic buildings to erase our mistakes.

I shake my head. I'm pretty surprised that these kids up here in Fort Collins have no idea who I am just by my face. I was all over the Denver news last spring. So were Ronin and Ford.

We fucked up. Bad. And the only reason we're not sitting in prison right now is because the cops in Boulder fucked up worse. They accessed one of Ford's computers illegally and obtained evidence that would put us away for a long time.

Luckily the grand jury was honest. They refused to allow that evidence and all the charges were dropped.

I let out a long breath at that. I hate thinking about it. It makes me sick. I close my eyes for a second to make those thoughts go away, and then continue playing nice with the art students. I love the art people. I'm a business major because my father was not about to pay exorbitant private university prices for an art degree. So we compromised. I'd take business—which I'm actually fucking stellar at—and he'd pay for a summer internship in France with a famous *trompe l'oeil* artist. That was two years ago. She taught me how to paint three dimensions in 2D and I used that to start my body art hobby.

I paint naked girls.

And that bombshell I'm waiting for, she's about to become my new canvas.

CHAPTER SIX

Veronica ditches me the second she leaves the art building. I let her go. I have a date with her at four anyway. Plus, she's done for the day. She only has one class, but I have three and mine are all across campus, so I have no time to stalk her ass or chase her down.

I walk out of finance class at three forty-five and smile all the way to my truck. Bomb's tattoo shop is just down the street, and technically I could probably walk to her shop faster than it takes me to get back to the parking lot over near the art building where my truck is. But that girl's coming home with me tonight. I'd hate for her little feet to become weary after hoofing it all the way across town to get to my truck.

I pull up in a space in front of Sick Boyz at three fifty-nine.

Her brother is waiting for me when I walk in, giving me a not-so-nice look. "Hey, man," I say casually. "What's up? I have an appointment with Veronica."

He gives me the once-over. Maybe the twice-over. He's a big guy. Bigger than me, and that's saying something. He might not be much taller, but his muscles say he works out daily. Possibly several times a day. He's wearing a white t-shirt with the shop logo on it—which is a rockabilly guy and a pin-up girl who could be a redhead version of his sister or a biker version of Jessica Rabbit. And both figures are tatted up and sitting on a badass bike. There's a few custom bikes out front, so I'm getting the feeling these guys are into the rides.

I make my befriend-the-brother move and stick out my hand to shake. He accepts it. "Spencer Shrike. That your chopper out there?"

He squeezes my hand, I squeeze back, then he drops it and nods. "Yup."

"Nice custom work, you do it yourself?"

"Yup."

"Cool, cool." I want to get more into it, talk about the custom shit my dad and me do, but something tells me he knows who I am and he's waiting for it. So I turn away and look at the pictures on the wall.

"I'm ready," Blondie says as she turns the corner of a hallway. "Follow me," she huffs as she turns her back and walks away.

I shoot Big Brother a smile, then do as I'm told. There are several tattoo rooms and hers is at the end. I watch her ass as she walks. She's wearing those scrubs that doctors wear in surgery. Hers are pink. That makes me smile. She looks like a pink girl. A real girly girl. I bet she wanted to be a princess when she grew up. She turns the corner into her room and beckons me inside with a sigh.

I stop short. "What the fuck?" Every surface of her room is covered in plastic. It's like the dentist, times a bazillion. The TV is covered, the chair is covered, the counters have plastic over them, and when I turn around to ask her what's up, she's got on a pink face mask. I laugh.

She flips me the finger. "Fuck you! You should be happy I'm so hygienic. You will never catch a disease in my room. Sit your ass down in the chair and don't say another word unless I ask you a question."

I chuckle under my breath and take a seat. The plastic crinkles underneath me and I slip around a little. "So, Veronica. I never properly introduced myself this morning. I'm Spencer."

"I don't need to know your name. Besides," she says as she slips a visor over her forehead that has a long clear plastic shield attached to it. "I already know all about you." Her last few words come out muffled and with an echo from behind the mask and the shield.

I smile and wink. "Don't believe everything you hear, then, OK?"

She ignores me. "Take your shirt off and tell me what you want that awful thing you're calling a tattoo turned into."

I slip my shirt over my head slowly, just like I did it this morning. She pretends to be busy with her machine and ink, but I catch her looking out of the corner of her eye. "I'm thinking I need a whole back piece to cover that little lady. I'm thinking ravens, and skulls, and smoke. I'm thinking Blackbirds, of the mechanical variety. I'm thinking all done up in black and red."

"Ha," she fake-laughs. "That's a month's worth of appointments. I want to know what you want me to do today."

"A Blackbird, Blondie. I want a Blackbird today. The hula girl can wait until we get the design right. Today I want you to start the piece. Give me that paper over there, I'll draw it out for you."

She looks at me skeptically, removes her face shield and mask and walks over to the counter top where she's got a spiral notebook. She grabs it, and a pen, even though there are pencils in the jar she's keeping her writing utensils in, and hands them over.

I open the notebook and realize it's her personal sketchbook. I look up at her and she's got her hands on her hips, like she's waiting on me to perform. I do the head-tilt smile and page through, trying to look at each of her drawings without being obvious. They are all very detailed with elaborate shading and perspective. She's a talented artist and I'm dying to see the sketch she did of me this morning.

I find a blank page and uncap the pen with my teeth and start to draw. I can sketch this image with my eyes closed, that's how often I've drawn it, both in real life and in my mind. I was drunk when I let Bobby Choo tat me up with a hula girl. Out-of-my-mind drunk, celebrating after the grand jury refused to indict me and my team for murder. That's the only way I'd let his dumb ass tat me up. Especially my first time. Because I've been planning this bike since I was a little kid and I was still handing my old man tools in our garage as he was building the business.

I'm not sure how much time goes by when Bomb whispers over my shoulder. "Thunderbird."

I laugh and turn my head. I don't have to turn it far, her cheek is practically right up against mine. "Yeah, baby. Thunderbird, American-style. The 1956 Triumph Blackbird. I want ravens and rooks. And skulls and smoke. All done up in black and red. But first, I want the Shrike Bikes version of the Blackbird. And this is it." I stop talking so I can stare at her lips for a moment. She licks them and I almost die. I reluctantly drag my eyes up to her heated stare. Her opinion of me has changed since I came in this room. I rip the page out of the notebook and set it on the counter. "Will you do it?"

She lets out a breath, like she was holding it in. "I'd need to plan it properly, Spencer."

The sound of my name coming out of her mouth gives me the chills. "Of course."

"You'd need to help me," she continues in a whisper.

"I'd have it no other way."

"I might need a model." She licks her lips again.

"I have the perfect specimen at home in my garage."

"You have a '56 Blackbird?"

"I do. You should come see it, get a feel for it between your legs. Get a feel for me as well."

She's undressing before my eyes. I almost have a heart attack and start looking for Monster Bro before I realize she's got shorts and a girly top on underneath her scrubs. Her hair comes down out of the pony tail and flows over her gorgeous breasts that are accentuated by the tightly stretched fabric of the Sick Boyz shirt. The next thing I know she's applying some red lip gloss and snapping her compact closed. "I'm ready."

"I have to admit," I say with an air of admiration as I slip my shirt back on. "I'm fucking impressed with that little display." I hold my hand out to her and she takes it, then snags the drawing up off the counter as I pull her out of the room and down the hall.

Monster Bro is about to bark at her when we appear holding hands, but Bombs just slaps the drawing down on the counter. "He's got this in his garage, he wants me to tattoo it on his back, so I'm going to see it in person."

Monster Bro is stunned silent so we make our escape and practically run to my truck. I open her door and she quickly slides in as I go around to my side. Her brother is just opening the door to object to what's happening when

I start up the truck, check for traffic, and pull out into the northbound lane of College Avenue.

"I live out in Bellvue, that OK?"

"Why would it be a problem?" She's got her foot up on the seat, her elbow propped on it, just looking at me. Whatever I did back in that shop, it changed her mind about me. And I'm not sure if it's the drawing or the fact that I have a '56 Bird in my garage, but at this point, I really do not care.

"You hardly know me. I'm taking you to a farmhouse in the middle of nowhere. I'm a known criminal."

She frowns. "So you are guilty?" It's a question, like she wants to believe I'm innocent, but she also wants to hear the truth.

"They dropped the charges for a reason, Bombshell. Let it go. I'm not the guy they made me out to be on the news. I'm not that guy."

She chews on her lip for a moment and then digs through her purse and pulls out her pink .38. "I've got my gun. So if you mess with me, I'll just put some bullets in it and make you sorry." She's laughing before she finishes her sentence.

I shake my head. "You should never carry an unloaded gun, Ronnie." She blushes at the nickname. I'm not sure why, I've got a shitload of nicknames for her a helluva lot more erotic than Ronnie. But I note this for future reference. "You might only get one chance to save your life with that gun. It needs to be loaded so when opportunity knocks, you're ready."

"I don't know how to shoot," she reluctantly admits after a few seconds' pause. "My dad and brothers never taught me. I bought the gun to piss them off, but I never learned how to shoot it. I don't even know what kind of bullets it takes. I've been wanting to learn for a long time though."

"Oh, baby," I say wistfully. This is a girl after my own heart. "You're talking to the right guy. I've got a shooting range on my property. I'll teach you the basics, then I'll put you on my gun club membership and buy you some marksmanship classes."

Her eyes light up. "OK," she says through her smile. "Wow." She laughs a little. "I think you just changed my life, Spencer Shrike."

"That was the plan, Bombshell. That was always the plan."

We drive in silence after that. She looks out the window as I make my way across the countryside until I come to my driveway. "Who do you live here with?" she asks as I pull past the house and park the truck next to the shop building out back.

"Just me. I inherited this house last year. I figure my life could use some slowing down, so I decided not to get an apartment near school and just drive in every day."

She jumps out, her hair waving in the wind. "What do you do out here all alone?" She follows me to the door and I unlock it and wave her through, flipping the switch for the lights as I pass in behind her.

She gasps in surprise as she takes in the room.

"I build bikes, Veronica Vaughn. I make custom bikes. You recognized a Triumph Thunderbird from a drawing, and at least one brother rides, so I know you have some knowledge about bikes. But what I don't know is if that interest is really you or just a byproduct of your upbringing."

Her fingertips caress the cherry-red tank on a custom piece I've been working on all summer and then she walks

49

straight over to the Blackbird and swings her leg over. She looks damn good on that bike. "I could ask you the same question, Spencer Shrike." She grips the handles and leans over like she's pretending to ride. How fucking cute is that?

"I learned to love them as a kid, but these bikes are my future. Can you ride?"

She shakes her head no. "My dad and brothers." This seems to be a common theme with her.

"So they run your life?"

"Yes," she laughs. "They do. I live at home. I don't make enough to move out and get my own place, I don't have a lot of clients yet. I just started at the shop a few weeks ago."

"Well, I can't blame them, really. If I had a sister as perfect as you, I'd never let her leave home or ride a bike either."

She smiles up at me from under her blonde hair. It's covering her bright blue eyes. "What about shoot a gun?"

I walk over to her and swing my leg over, sitting behind her. She hisses out an exhale, like I just surprised her. When I wrap my arms around her waist, she moans. "Guns are a lot safer than bikes, Ronnie," I whisper in her ear. "Shooting is something you should know how to do." I flatten my hands against her belly, then slip them inside the bottom of her tank top.

She draws in a breath.

"Do you want me to stop, Ronnie?"

Veronica hesitates and I pull back, but her hands grab mine and hold them to her body, tightly. "No, I don't want you to stop." She looks over her shoulder at me, her mouth open, her chest rising and falling faster than it was a few seconds ago.

I lean into her neck and kiss the soft skin, right under her ear.

She shudders.

"Oh, hell," she sighs. "Maybe you should stop."

I pull back immediately. "I will if you really want me to. But Veronica—" I reach up to turn her chin towards me. She has to reposition herself a little to look me in the eye. "Don't say no because it's expected of you. Or because you're afraid I might hurt you. Or because it's too soon. Because you're mine, baby. I knew the moment I saw you last week, outside the bookstore having it out with your brother over something. I watched you stand your ground and toss your hair at the same time. And I told myself, *She's mine. I need her. I don't know her, but I will.* And now I do. And I want you. Not just for tonight, not for just a weekend, not for just this semester to pass the time, not just to get some kickass ink on my body. I want you for all those things, but I want them indefinitely."

She lets out a long breath. "Holy shit, that's sorta deep. What's that even mean? Indefinitely?"

"It means I'm here, for as long as you want me."

"But you don't even know me, Spencer."

"I've watched you for weeks. I know all I need to know."

She's silent for a moment, and then she stands up and turns around and straddles the long black leather seat, facing me. "What do you want me to say?"

I smile. "When I ask if I can touch you tonight, I want you to say yes. When I ask if I can kiss you tonight, I want you to say yes. When I ask if I can have you tonight, I want you to say yes. Just say yes, Ronnie. I want you to say yes. One word, that's it. One word is all it takes. And I really will change your life."

Her eyes dart back and forth, searching my face. I can almost hear her thoughts. Running all the questions through her mind, past conventional expectations. Past her father's opinion of her. Past her brothers' reactions if they find out she gave in to me after knowing me less than twenty-four hours.

And then she closes her eyes and whispers, "Yes."

I rub her bare thighs, causing her to shiver, and then I grab the hem of her tank top and lift it over her head, revealing her breasts, perfectly cradled inside a lacy pink bra. "I knew it would be pink," I whisper as I toss the shirt and pull her chest right up to mine. "I've pictured you in this moment a thousand times over the past few weeks, and those fantasies don't even come close to how beautiful you look to me right now."

Her perfectly manicured fingernails grab the hem of my shirt next. I let her do it herself because she drags those nails up my abs and then pushes it over my head, leaning in, pressing her breasts up against me. I grab her around the waist again, pulling her fully into me, my mouth on hers, probing with my tongue. She parts her lips, allowing me entrance, suddenly panting from her rapidly racing heart.

My hand goes to her chest so I can feel the thumping I've created, then I slip her bra down over her soft mounds and squeeze. "Your tits are fucking fabulous. I'd like to stick my dick between them and fuck your mouth at the same time."

She gasps as her eyebrows hike up. "Oh, my God!"

"Do you like the dirty talk, Bombshell? Does it turn you on?"

She looks like she wants to reply, but words evade her, so she simply nods.

"I'll keep it to myself if it bothers you, but you should know, my mind will be thinking these dirty things every time I'm around you, Bombshell. Because once I have this"—I look hungrily down at her body—"I'll never forget it. I will undress you, reliving the scent of your pussy, every time I see you. My fingers will be reliving how I make your nipples bunch up against my touch. My cock will be reliving how good it feels when you clamp yourself around me."

"Oh, my God!" she moans. "Don't stop talking. Holy fuck, Spencer. Please, don't stop! I like it."

I unbutton her little jean shorts and smack her thigh. "Stand up and take these off."

She stands up and swings her leg over the bike seat, then shimmies her hips until the shorts fall to the ground around her wedge-heeled sandals. She kicks them off to the side and stands in front of me. "Now you, Spencer."

I shoot her a crooked, devious, filthy grin. "Now me, what?" I growl. "If you want something from me, you have to ask for it. And if you expect me to deliver, you better be descriptive."

She blushes and my wood is petrified, that's how fucking hard I am for this girl. She doesn't ask, she just takes. She slips out of her panties and straddles the bike again, her legs open and her wet pussy exposed. She goes for the button on my jeans and I stop her hand.

"You want my cock, Ronnie? You want me to take it out and fuck your tits and your mouth?"

She pants harder now. "Yes."

"Say it, Bomb. Tell me why you want it, or I won't give it to you. I'll tease you and leave you to suffer. If you want me, you have to ask for it. You have to ask for it the exact way you want it, Veronica. If you want my cock in your mouth, tell me. If you want my cock between your perfect tits, say it. If you want to suck me until I come down your throat—fuck, baby. Just ask. I'm ready."

She stares up at me, her ragged breath a total betrayal of her desires. But I stay still and quiet as I wait her out.

"I want you," she finally whispers. "I want—" She stops to swallow hard and closes her eyes. Her cheeks flush red with embarrassment, but she forces the words out anyway. "I want your cock between my tits, Spencer. I want you to fuck me in my mouth." She squeezes her tits together and wiggles her pussy against the hard thickness pressing up against my jeans.

I can't take the restraint anymore, so I get off the bike and strip off the jeans. I'm still commando from this morning's modeling job, and His Highness is ready for battle. I sit back down and look down at her pussy. It's so wet her juices are almost flowing out onto the black leather bike seat. I grab her hips and pull, bringing her beckoning sex within easy reach of my throbbing cock. "Lie back, baby. I'm gonna take you now. I'll get to your tits and your mouth later, but right now I'm gonna fuck you good. I'm gonna make you squirt. Are you a squirter, Bombshell?" I push her until she falls back against the tank. "I bet I can find out right now." I slip two fingers inside her and thrust, fast and hard. She buckles and screams, wiggling against my palm, which probably stimulates her more. I pull my fingers out quickly once her muscles begin to clamp. "You are, baby. You are most definitely a squirter. But I'm not gonna let you off that easy. If you want that, you can ask for it next time."

"Oh. My God," seems to be her standard answer tonight. I've got her off balance. She's not sure what to make of me, but her wet pussy says she's OK with that for now. I ease forward and she moans out, "Please, Spencer, just fuck me! Please!"

I do fuck her on the '56 Blackbird. She screams my name four times. We almost topple the damn thing over with our antics and I could care less. That bike can be repaired, but this first dirty fuck with my Bombshell, that's never gonna happen again.

It's a once-in-a-lifetime thing.

It's a change-my-life-forever thing.

It's a falling-in-love-and-lust thing.

It's a recognizing-my-best-friend thing.

And it's the day I decide—this girl is mine.

Forever.

CHAPTER SEVEN

I pull myself out of the past and sigh. It's not going to end this way, that's for damn sure. It's not. I've been planning for my moment for years and that shit is just about in reach. I refuse to submit to circumstances.

I glance up at the clock on the wall and realize it's already ten o'clock. I might as well go back into town early, just in case Ronnie thinks she can duck out and evade me at closing time. I grab my keys and my phone and head down to the buildings on the far end of the property where I keep the surveillance van. Ford's robot shit is in there and I won't have time to come back to the house before meeting him at midnight.

I key open the garage and walk into the darkness. A stray beam from the outside security light bounces off a chrome fender and distracts me for a moment. I reach over to the wall and flip on the light.

My old Chevy truck—the same one I drove around town when I first moved out here, the same one I met Ronnie in—is staring back at me. One of my mechanics borrowed it last week when his truck was out of commission. He must've parked it in the wrong bay.

I suddenly have an overwhelming need to drive this truck into town to see Ronnie. Maybe I can talk her into going for a drive and it will spark a memory in her? A memory that reminds her that we're good together. I fish around in a drawer where I keep an extra set of keys, then reach inside the surveillance van and pull out Ford's case. I think there's a computer in there, but I really have no idea. He locks that shit up tight. It's not really a briefcase, it's a portable safe. You'd break whatever's inside opening it up without a key, and even if you ever did access Ford's computer, he's got an automatic kill switch on the drive if you get the password wrong just once. We learned our lesson the last time his shit was breached. Almost cost us life in prison. We don't make the same mistakes twice so the password kill is more than a just-in-case precautionary measure. And Ford never forgets a password. There is no need for a second chance.

I check the back of the van for anything else we might need, but it's clean back here, so I get in the old Chevy, set the case down on the passenger seat, and pull out of the garage.

The ride back into FoCo is nothing but a whole lot of time to stew in all the mistakes I've made over the past few years. I'm second-guessing everything. The team, the jobs, the revenge, the bailouts. All of it had consequences we never saw coming.

But there's nothing we can do about that now. We just need to move forward and clean it up as best we can.

The only thing I don't regret is how I've handled Ronnie. In her case, I did everything right. I made sure of it. I covered all my tracks, I left no trace, I have kept her as far from me as possible for as long as possible. New Year's was the first time I slept with her in months. And that was a private party. We stayed the night in Rook's old garden apartment. We never left the building together. I made sure I was gone in the morning when she woke up.

The time before that it was just after Rook spilled her guts about her life on national TV and got more than a hundred people arrested in the process. People lined up outside Chaput Studios with giant signs. One proclaimed her a lying whore. And that was one of the nicer signs. She wasn't even living there, she was here with me. But as soon as those monsters found that out, they parked at the end of my driveway.

I smile. They made the mistake of assuming that the road leading up to my house was public. It's not. It's my road, all three miles of it. It's on my fucking land, which makes that land my fucking home. Which means I can shoot those fuckers if the right situation arises and it's totally legal according to Colorado law.

I never got my chance to shoot anyone, but I did beat the shit out of a reporter who was hiding in the trees near the river in back of my house.

The county deputies pretty much had it after that. They cleared them all out under the pretense that it was a fire hazard. A few years ago this whole area was up in flames, so people tend to take that fire talk seriously around here.

Rook survived. Ford was here, Ronin was here. The Biker Channel hired security. She never had to leave if she didn't want to, she worked in my shop while we were filming and did her classes online. Ford fired that piece-of-shit tutor who ratted us out and helped Rook in her college math class himself. I even got Ronin to do her delivery duties.

We protected her one hundred percent. But her situation was unique.

For instance, Ronnie works in a tattoo shop downtown. If she doesn't work, she doesn't make money. She can't pay her bills. Her family is not rich. Hell, they're not even middle-class. They might be the token white trash of Fort Collins. They do have a big-ass house in the historic district, but they have that house for one reason only—Gramps won it in a poker game back in 1958. It's not in good repair. The place is freezing-ass cold in the winter because the furnace is so old it hardly functions, and the roof has been leaking since I met her.

And Ronnie might have a pack of badass brothers and a father who'd drop you with one kick to the throat, but the doors don't even lock on that house. The windows barely shut. The only reason it's never been robbed is because the Vaughn clan scares the shit out of people.

If Ronnie was thrust into the public eye like Rook was, she'd never make it. The entire family would be annihilated. They'd lose their business, they'd be hounded day and night. And there's no way to restrict picketers on a public sidewalk in downtown like I can do on my little backcountry private road.

There's just no way to keep her safe other than the way I've been doing it. Ignoring her.

The minute anyone finds out this girl is my future Mrs. Spencer Shrike, people will pounce. And while I can handle that at any other time—I could get her out of here and put her somewhere safe, I could make sure the Vaughn clan gets Sick Boyz' rent paid on time, I could drum up business for them with some word-of-mouth buzz—I cannot do any of that shit right *now*.

We've got a major trial happening in two weeks. Rook will need to testify about the most horrific details of her previous life. They will try their best to link Ronin, Ford, and myself to a shitload of crimes that took place several years ago. I cannot be worrying about Ronnie and her family.

It's just not a good time.

I turn off College Avenue before I get to Ron's shop and park the truck on Maple, right next to my new building. It used to be an auto repair place a few years ago, but that went under and no one picked it back up. The Biker Channel loved the location, just past all the cute shops in downtown so we won't offend anyone with our loud bikes. Plus, it's already set up for a shop.

I get out of the truck and walk up to it, just checking shit out. The windows are all boarded up still. No one's supposed to see inside until the grand opening and the crews won't even start painting the outside for another week.

Not much to see, so I head down the street towards Sick Boyz. It's still packed when I get there. All those frat guys are milling about outside waiting on their brothers to be finished. They're drunk and I don't like it.

I check my phone for the time. Ten forty-five. And just as I look up, Ronnie comes plowing through the doors in a rush. I slink back against the building, hiding in the crowd of guys as she looks up and down the street, probably checking to see if I'm doing recon on her ass. One of the guys outside the shop whistles at her and she flips him the bird and tells him to fuck off as she walks off towards home.

I start to laugh, but it dies in my throat because she stops at Mountain Avenue and hits the walk button. This is where things get interesting. Because her house is west, and that signal is for crossing College Avenue to the east.

JA HUSS

My legs are in motion before my brain fully understands what's happening. I'm an act-now-think-later kinda guy, so I take off after her. Where the fuck is she going? It's late, it's dark, she's got no car—she should not be walking around downtown alone. Not that this town is unsafe *per se*, but bad shit happens everywhere. Even here. And it's a college town, which means there's always the threat of predators.

She walks briskly on Mountain, then turns abruptly into an alley. I hang back. My Ronnie is not stupid. She never looked back at me, but I taught her to keep walking if she ever thought she was being followed. Keep quiet for as long as possible and get that gun ready. I stalk up to the corner and wait. I know she's on the other side, ready to pounce on anyone who appears. I can feel her when she's this close. Like we're connected. I can almost hear her heartbeat, that wild heartbeat that drives me crazy beating against mine as she lies on top of me after sex.

I hear an exhale, then the pounding of her Chucks as she beats a retreat. I poke my head around and catch her disappearing around another corner. But this is not a street, it's a building. I cross the alley and stalk the wall, getting to her corner just in time to hear a screen door slam.

What the fuck is she doing?

I peak around the corner just as some lights flip on in an upstairs apartment over an old building.

That little sneak got her own place. Her car is out back, parked. And sure enough, there's a For Sale sign on it. And she's dating some rich guy. I bet she's got new panties on as well! That uptight fuckass banker is enjoying my Bomb's new panties!

I'll kill him.

I walk over to the stairs and try my best to be quiet as I ascend, but they are wooden. And old. And squeaky. Suddenly the door is kicked open and a gun is pressing against my cheek. "Move one inch, motherfucker. I'll blow your teeth out the other side of your head!"

"Whoa there, Ron, it's me, baby."

She pulls the gun off my face. "Holy hell, Spencer! You scared the fuck out of me! I thought you were gonna break in and rape me!"

"Well…" I chuckle a little. She does not find my joke funny. At all. "Sorry, Veronica. I was waiting for you outside the shop and saw you walking the wrong direction. I just needed to see what's up."

"It's none of your business what I do." She pulls the screen door open and walks into her place.

I follow her in and stalk her to the kitchen, where she grabs a beer from the fridge and then pushes past me and plops herself down on the raggedy thing some might call a couch.

"So… you moved out? Why? And what's this shit about you selling your car? I bought you that for graduation. "

She kicks her Chucks up on the battered coffee table and twists off her beer cap. "I'm twenty-three, Spencer. It's about time I left the nest, don't you think?"

"Uh…" No, not really. That's not what I think at all. I like her at home. I like her surrounded by Gramps and her father and little brother. Three related men in the house. Yes, that's something I can live with for a long time, thank you. But I say none of that. My Shrike Sense is tingling. I feel a declaration of independence coming from my little Ron. So I sit down next to her and try to be

63

reasonable. "Ronnie, this place is a dump. You can't stay here."

She takes a swig of her Fat Tire and lets out a long, "Ahhhhh." Totally ignoring me.

I decide on the subtle approach. "So how long is the lease? Please tell me it's a month-to-month."

She flips the TV to Comedy Central. There's an *Ab Fab* marathon and I get a little distracted for a second. But then I snap out of it and take my attention back to her. "Veronica, answer me. Why are you living in this dump?"

She laughs as Patsy smokes a joint on TV, then drags her eyes over to me. "If you're here to fuck me tonight, the answer is no. I have a boyfriend."

"What? Yeah, me! I'm the boyfriend!" I stand up and pace. This has gone too far now. "Please tell me you're not seeing that banker asshole. Because I swear—"

"Dammit! Who told you that? Ford? Did Ford tell you? I'll kill his ass."

"I saw you together at dinner, Veronica. What the fuck is up? And I still want to know why the fuck you're living in this alleyway shithole."

She snorts out a laugh and shakes her head. "You have no clue, Spencer. None." She looks over at me again, only now her eyes are filled with anger. "You really think that you can saunter in here and demand my attention?" She stands up and points at me. "You really think I give a fuck what you think about my home? Fuck you. I'm not ashamed of this place." She looks around the apartment and points to the art affixed to the walls with thumb tacks, and then looks back at me. "I love this place. I *love* this place," she repeats with the emphasis. "You wanna know why I love this dumpy little shithole? I'll tell you. It's because it's *my* dumpy fucking shithole, you giant prick. I

64

wasn't born to a wealthy family. I wasn't given a private education growing up. I didn't even have a fucking mother, you insensitive jerk. I had to claw my way through dinner every night. Fighting back four brothers for food. I had to submit to them at every turn. I had to fight them, for fuck's sake. When they got the itch to pick on me, whether it was in play or not. My life has been nothing but one long fucking struggle. And this"—she pans her hands wide to include all the space within her little apartment— "this is my reward. And maybe it's not up to your goddamned standards, but no one gives a fucking shit about you in this room except *you*, Spencer Shrike. And you do not deserve me. You don't. I'm a good person. I worked hard to get what I have. And maybe it's not a lot compared to what you have, but at least I got it honestly."

I just stare at her. Unable to move or even form a sentence.

"So fuck off. I've moved on, asshole. Get it through your thick skull. I'm not interested."

"Veronica," I say calmly. "You don't—"

My cheek is suddenly stinging with heat and Veronica is staring at her red palm, stunned that it actually struck out and hit me across the face.

She shakes herself out of her daze and points her finger at me again. "Don't you dare tell me what I think or what I feel. Don't you dare. I'm so fucking tired of people telling me things about myself they have no clue about. Every damn day I walk into Sick Boyz and swallow down the vomit. Do you know that about me, Spencer? You think you know me so well. Do you know that the smell of blood makes me sick? The sight of blood makes me sick? Not sick as in I might faint, or I might feel a little queasy, or that's sorta gross. But sick in a way that makes my heart beat so fast I think I might drop dead. It gives me panic attacks, Spencer. Every damn day I fight it off." Her whole body is shaking.

"Ronnie—" But I have nothing to say. "I didn't know that, no. I thought you liked it. It's art."

"*Art*?" She laughs and then the tears spill out. "Art? It's a fucking tattoo shop, you dumbass! I went to school for four years to study art and three years later I trace line drawings on skin. I have to cover myself head to toe in personal protection equipment because I am obsessed with the idea that I'll contract hepatitis through some innocuous cut on my arm. Did you ever once ask me why I cover the room in plastic?"

She stops her rant to let me think about this. Have I? "I don't need to ask, Ronnie. I know why."

"Why? Tell me why, then, if you're so fucking smart."

"You hate the blood and—"

"Wrong." She cuts me off. "That's not why. Do you realize no one—*no one*," she reiterates—"has ever asked me why I cover the room in plastic?"

I move towards her to bring her in my arms. She struggles against me but I'm so much bigger, it's hardly a problem. I wrap her up and pull her close to my chest so I can lean down in her ear and whisper, "You cover the room in plastic to protect people, Veronica. I've always known that was the reason."

She starts to cry and I just hold her close. This is an end-of-the-line meltdown my little Ronnie is having. She's good and strung out. Bad.

"I don't want to go there anymore, Spencer. I need this, OK? I need this so fucking bad. I can't think straight when I'm at work. All I see is the blood. And I finally have a chance to make a real change. This banker, Spencer. He's my chance. Please don't ruin it for me."

We stand there in silence for a few moments. I'm not enough for her right now, I can see that now. I can't give her what she needs because of my own stupid mistakes. This is her personal struggle and it's got nothing to do with me. "What do you want me to do, Ronnie?" And even though I already know what she's gonna say, it hurts me so fucking bad when the words finally come out.

"Leave me alone, Spencer. Just go. Leave me alone."

I swallow hard and shake my head. She doesn't try and pull away, she gives me this moment at least. "Veronica, if that's what you need, I'll go. But before I do, I'd like to have my say too." She stays silent so I push forward. "The day I saw you, my life started. My chest swelled with this feeling. A feeling I'd never felt before. When I watched you that first week before I made my move in art class, I realized something. I realized that the day I saw you my heart started to beat a whole new way. It was like all these years I had no idea what my heart was for, and then bam—you were there in front of me. And by the time I followed you to art class that day we got together, I had finally figured out what it was."

I blow out a long burst of air, not sure I should even be telling her this.

"Say the words, Spencer," she pleads through her soft sobs. "Because if I don't hear them, I'm gonna explode."

Her eyes are searching mine, pleading to make this better. Just begging me to fix this.

"It was like… it was like…" I take a deep breath. "It was like I was listening to some scratchy classic vinyl and then suddenly you appeared, and my whole world went digital. It's like life *shifted*. Everything became real. You make me real, Ronnie. You started my heart. You are the missing piece of me. We're partners, Ron. Soul mates. We are, I swear it. But—" She cries into my chest again and it stops me dead. I can't stand to see her cry. God, it hurts me to see her cry.

"I can't listen to the 'but', Spencer. I can't. Please don't make me listen to the 'but'. I just want you to say you love me."

"I love you, Veronica. I've always loved you."

She looks up at me, her eyes all red and watery. "Then *be* with me! Please!"

Fuck, her misunderstood sadness breaks my heart. "I want to say I'm with you, baby. I'll never leave you. But I can't say that. Not yet."

"Why?" She's a mess now. Her tears are spilling down her face like mad.

She pulls away and I bring her back. My hand comes up to cup her face. I tilt her chin up so she has to look me in the eyes when the words come out. "Because Veronica Vaughn, I'm guilty. Every single thing they said about me on TV that year I met you..." I pause to try and gauge her reaction. But I have no idea what she's thinking, so I have no choice, I just have to say it. "Every single thing they said about me was true."

I can hear her stunned swallow and then she wriggles until I let her go.

And I do let her go. I have to let her go.

"It's all true, Ronnie. So if you need this banker to get what you want, then go do that. Because I am *this guy*, Veronica. This guy right here, this guy who did all those things all those years ago. This guy is me. And you're absolutely right. This guy doesn't deserve you."

CHAPTER EIGHT

I have to walk away, so I turn towards the door.

"Spencer," she whispers.

"Veronica, I'm sorry, OK? I just need to go." I pull the screen door open and walk though, taking the steps two at a time, and then walk briskly around the corner of her building. When I get to the alley I lean against the wall and bend over to try and calm my racing heart. "Fuck!"

She probably heard that. I stand back up and walk down the alley towards Mountain Ave, then cut over and take Jefferson back up to Maple where my truck is parked at the shop. If she stays in that apartment at least she'll be close to me.

When I get to the truck I just sit there, trying to process what my life will be like without her around the edges. Frayed. That's what my life will be. Even though she wasn't in my life all the time, everything I did, everything I do, I do with her in mind. Every decision I make. Every person I spend time with. Every cent I spend. The first thing I do is ask myself, is this good for *us*? Will this make Ronnie and me stronger in the end? Will this make her happy?

I punch the steering wheel and my knuckles split open. "Fuck." My phone rings and I pull it out of my pocket. "Ford," I say. "On my way, dude."

I hang up before he can say anything and start the truck, then I head west and cut over to Mountain Avenue. Ford lives down the street from Ronnie's family house, in an old Victorian across from City Park.

He's waiting on the corner of Mountain and Frey so I pull over. He's dressed up in dark jeans and a black t-shirt, looking like a cat burglar. He pulls the door open and slides in. "Where's the fucking van? I have shit—" He sees the case on the floor. "Well, that does not explain why you're driving your personal vehicle while we're doing a job, Spencer."

"I just wanted to, Ford. No reason." I follow the road past his house and look hard at it. "You sneaking out tonight? That tiny wife of yours cracking the whip already?"

He flashes me a sardonic glare. "Right. The fucking dogs will hear the vehicle and have a hissy fit if you came to the house at night."

"Dogs?" I almost choke. "Since when are you an animal person?"

"I've always loved pets, Spencer," he says with a grin. And then he laughs that diabolical laugh of his and growls, "Don't be an idiot. They're not really *dogs*, they're employees. Security. I paid forty grand apiece for these fucking dogs. One wrong look at Ashleigh or Kate and they eat your face off."

"That does not sound safe, Ford."

"I'm half kidding. We had them trained and bonded specifically to us while we were in New Zealand. They are the best-behaved employees I've ever had." He stops for a moment. "Aside from Pam, of course. I cannot allow Ash or Kate to be hurt because our past is rushing up to greet us. I wanted to send them away, but I'd go out of my mind with worry if I didn't know where they were at all times. So I got dogs. They have service jackets, they can go anywhere a human can and they are trained to work as a team. One dog attacking you is frightening, two are formidable."

"I'd just give her a gun, Ford. Quicker and no shit to clean up."

"She has a gun, Spencer. But when you've got a baby in your arms, a gun is not practical."

"Security guard?"

"I have those too, but they need to stay hidden. Ashleigh has no idea what we're really into, Spencer, so keep your fucking mouth shut. I've got it all under control. We've moved into a normal house and I want them to have a normal life."

"Nice house, by the way. How the hell did you get all that shit organized from New Zealand? You've only been back for like three days."

"Pam."

"That personal assistant chick? Must be nice, eh? Have her to take care of things for you."

"It is, Spence. You know the Biker Channel wants you to get one, right? They've been hounding me about it for weeks. They say you hardly ever answer their calls and ignore the emails completely. You should just hire someone to take care of that shit."

"Yeah," I say. "Maybe I should. I could use the help. How close do you need me to be, Ford?" I hang a right on Elizabeth and then cut up north to where Drake's shop is.

71

"Just about the same place we were before. I didn't get the long-range option for this bot. That model was out of stock." He pulls the case up from the floor, keys in his passcode to disengage the locks, and then pops it open. When I glance over he's got a tablet in there and some smaller things tucked away in a bulging pocket on the inside of the lid. He fires up the tablet and then accesses some app on the home screen that controls the bot. A camera pops up in a new window, but the image is black.

"Night vision is standard," Ford says. Like I was actually wondering how much he pays for the fucking robot add-ons. "OK, here we go." The bot screen flashes green, and then some details start to emerge. "We're under a workbench, I think. Hold on, let me look around a little and see if this is acceptable. You might have to tell me where a good place will be, Spencer. A place that's in plain view, but not near something he needs every day. I don't mind losing the money I paid for this should things go bad. But I certainly don't want this bot in the hands of that stupid fuck Drake. He will blab all over about it and even though I had Merc cover my tracks, Homeland will be called in and they will immediately know it was me. I'm already on a list for hacking."

I wince. We're doing this job because I asked for it. "Maybe we should just pull it, then, Ford? Maybe I should just eat the money and drop it. He won't last, I'm not really worried about him taking my business, I'm just excitable. I'm an artist. People buy my bikes because I made them. And he's not me."

Ford just stares at me. "Who are you?"

"I'm serious, Ford. Let's just come back tomorrow and—" A knock on the glass stops me cold and Ford's eyes dart to the window behind me. "Please tell me that's not the pigs," I say without turning my head to look.

Ford laughs under his breath. "It's Drake."

I turn in my seat so I can see and then slide the window down about an inch. "Can I help you?" I ask, peering out at him.

He's not as tall as me when I'm standing, so when I'm sitting in a big-ass truck, he looks minuscule. He's such a skinny little fuck.

He scowls at me, squinting his eyes as he tries to make out if it's really me behind the tinted glass window. "Shrike? I should've known. You're out here like a loser, spying on me? What the hell?"

"I'm sorry," I say politely. "Do I know you?" Ford chuckles off to my right. "Do we know this rat, Ford?" I lower the window another half an inch. "Oh, wait," I say sarcastically. "Yeah, we know this asshole. He's the poser who moved into my town, pretending to be me. You're not even worth my time, Fonzie." I catch the sound of the little bot being maneuvered from the tablet.

Drake squints his eyes and gives those thick black frames a push up his nose as he considers this. "Then would you care to explain why you're sitting outside my shop in the middle of the night?"

"We're smoking a doobie, Drake. And you're killing my fucking buzz, so shoo, little man. Just shoo."

Ford laughs again.

Drake sniffs the air, trying to smell me out. "You're not smoking in there."

"It's that new odorless blend out of Boulder, you idiot. Now scram."

Ford bursts out laughing, "Scram," he mutters. "What are you, a character in *Scooby-Doo*?"

I look over at him and laugh. "Yeah, scram. That's such a great word, isn't it? So underused." I turn back and Drake is still there. "Drake, if you have an opinion on the merits of the word 'scram', let's hear it. Otherwise, get the fuck out of here."

He does that little two-finger to the eyeballs gesture, pointing at me, then his peepers, and I laugh like a girl.

"I'm watching you, Shrike. I know you're up to something and if I catch you around my shop, I'll take care of business."

I roll the window back up as Drake walks away. "You get it parked, dude?"

"We're set," Ford says. "He really is annoying. I'm pretty sure he's not your guy though, Spencer. He's so stupid. How the hell did he get past your security outside the showroom, let alone move seven bikes through the back fucking door? It makes no sense. This guy is backed, that's for sure. But he's not the one who stole your shit."

"Maybe not. But he's part of it, whether he knows that or not. Whoever is behind Drake Cikes is my guy. And I'm not sure who that might be, but I'm gonna figure it out."

I pull the truck forward, do the double honk to Drake—who is still standing in the alleyway entrance to his shop—and turn right at the next street to go back towards town.

Ford lets out a huff as he thinks in silence for a few seconds. "I might've been wrong earlier. This might be something after all. And I'm with you on figuring it out. Maybe it's not connected to the trials coming up. Maybe Drake is just some guy who fell into some money and decided to give you a run for yours. And maybe those missing bikes are just bad luck on your part. Some past employee getting revenge or some shit like that."

I look over at him as I wait for the light at Mountain and College.

"But somehow I doubt it. I think whoever is backing Drake is absolutely the one we should be looking at about the missing bikes. But I also think that somehow, some way, all of this is tied to Rook."

"Rook?"

"Yeah," he sighs. "They might be sending messages. And your bikes might've just been the initial greeting."

We sit in silence as I make my way back down Mountain to Ford's house. I pull over at the corner of Frey, and he opens the truck door. "Just keep an eye out, Spencer. And for fuck's sake, don't do anything stupid without calling Ronin and me first."

I laugh. "Yeah, if we do something stupid, we should definitely do it together."

"That's what teams are for, brother."

"Later, dude. Tell your little dudettes I said hey."

He flashes me a two-finger salute and slams the door closed. I watch him walk up to the house and when he gets to the porch, the light flicks on. Ashleigh appears and for a minute I expect them to fight. I really did figure he had to sneak out to do this shit tonight. But she leans up on her tiptoes and plants a kiss on his cheek. He smiles broadly, and then ushers her back inside and the porch light goes dark.

I sigh.

How ironic is it that Ford has a fucking family before the rest of us? And even Ronin has Rook. At least he has her.

Me? I have no one.

CHAPTER NINE

I park the truck over by the shop and walk back down to Ronnie's alley once again. I know this is probably the wrong thing to do, but I can't help myself. When I reach the parking area below her apartment, I lean against the wall of the building next door and I dial her number.

She's awake, I know that for sure, even though it's almost one AM and all the lights are off save for the flickering bluish tint that comes from a TV. It rings. One… if she doesn't pick up I'll leave. Two… if she doesn't pick up, I'll go knock on the door. Three… her shadow walks across in front of the apartment window.

"What do you want, Spencer?" she answers curtly.

I swallow down the feelings her words evoke. Because it's crystal clear that she's really done with me.

"Hey, uh…" I clear my throat. "I've been thinking, ya know. How you work so hard and everything." I pause to see if she'll say anything. But all I hear is her soft breath. "And I was just talking to Ford. You know how he has that assistant who's been working for him in LA?"

"Spencer, get to the point, OK? I'm tired."

"Pam, right? You remember me talking about Pam? She works for Ford long-distance. You know, she does everything virtually. They almost never see each other."

"I'm hanging up."

"Bombshell, please." I hear a smile on the other end, I know it. "Just calm the fuck down for a minute, OK? I'm trying to tell you something."

She walks past the window again, then pulls the sheer curtains aside and peeks out. The moonlight hits her face and illuminates her blue eyes for a second before she drops the curtain and walks away. "Just tell me then, Spencer. I'm tired."

"Pam works as Ford's personal assistant. She runs his email and shit. Schedules things and, well, shit like that. You get it?"

She huffs. "Spencer, I know what a PA does, just fucking spit it out. What's Pam got to do with this conversation?"

"Ford and Pam go way back. Since college. But the Biker Channel has a budget for a PA, so she got a raise when he started working for them. They have a small budget for each of us. Rook included. And they've been on me for a while to hire someone since I ignore them most of the time. And I was wondering if you'd like the job?"

She laughs. "You're kidding me, right?"

"It's not a huge deal, my budget is only forty grand a year—"

"No, thank you."

"—and benefits—"

"No."

"—and paid holidays."

"I said no, Spencer. I'm not interested."

"It starts next Monday. Hours are variable—"

"What fucking part of 'no' do you not understand?"

"I'd need you on call almost all the time, but I wouldn't be unreasonable, ya know?"

"I'm really hanging up now."

"I'd let you do your thing. Work the tattoo shop. Or—" I stop to wait and see if she's gonna hang up. But I hear her breathing. "Or whatever else you'd like to do. You could quit the shop, Ronnie."

Silence.

"You could do something else. Date someone else. Start a new life, if that's what you want. I won't interfere."

I get the three quick beeps that says the call is dead and I look up at her window. She paces back and forth a few times, and then her shadow disappears. There's no more movement, but the TV stays on.

I sit out there for more than an hour, leaning back against the wall. Watching her get up and occasionally grace me with a shadow. And at two thirty the place finally goes dark and I walk back to my shop. I open the side door, go inside, and flip on the lights.

This place is my dream realized. Everything in this shop is all I've ever wanted in a bike business. There's six bays with bike lifts, custom tool kits with more than a hundred thousand dollars in equipment. The cinder block walls are painted red and black and there are reproductions of my tattoos covering every inch. Blackbirds, rooks, crows, and ravens. Everywhere.

Ronnie says she traces line drawings on skin. Fuck, she could not be more wrong. To me, the art on my body is just as beautiful as any classical piece hanging in a museum. Veronica Vaughn is the Renoir of the tattoo world.

I walk past Rook's reception area. She's gonna run the showroom and the desk this season and she won't be answering calls. The showroom is open to the public, but bike appointments won't be made over the phone. In fact, we've got the entire year scheduled. Everyone had to put up a fifty grand deposit to get a Shrike bike this year and Season Two will tape on and off for almost six months instead of the three months we've been doing. We'll deliver a new bike to one high-profile customer each episode, and we'll do that twelve times.

This is it. This is what it looks like.

Success.

My eyes sweep to my office door and I walk past the reception area towards it. My name is on the door, done up in the fancy Shrike Bikes font. Yeah, I have my own font. People will be able to download it for free from the website. I open the heavy maple door and wave my hand in front of the light sensor so I can take a good long look at my future. I turn back to my bay, which is even more tricked out with a custom-airbrushed tool chest that has the Shrike Raven painted on the front.

I turn back to the office and walk around the massive stainless steel table that's been custom-fabricated and welded into my throne. This is where I'm going. This is where I've been headed since I turned eighteen and decided I would take this business over. This is the pinnacle of my dream.

And for some reason, it's just not that sweet.

I drop down into the soft black leather chair. It's so fucking luxurious I actually feel myself relax.

But none of this means anything to me right now. Because the only reason I was working so hard towards this future was so I could share it with Ronnie.

And she wants out. She's done. I see it. I'm not delusional. I'm not one of those guys who wants to force himself on a woman and make her submit to his advances. Trick her into telling him how she feels, how she can't live without him.

I'm not like that. I want my Ronnie, but I only want her if she wants me.

And right now, she hates my fucking guts.

I lean back in my chair, looking up at the ceiling. Thinking about how this might go.

I snap back to the present after a while and reach into my pocket for Carson Reed's ID. He lives up north, not that far from me actually, but in a new neighborhood filled with those up-and-coming professional types.

Carson Reed is the key, I figure. I get up and walk back into the reception area, then scribble a note on the work order board telling the guys I won't be in tomorrow. Today. When I look up at the new Shrike Bikes clock with my face staring back at me, it's just about four in the morning.

They can live without me for one day, because I've got business to take care of.

CHAPTER TEN

I sit inside the backseat and just bide my time, tired as fuck, but amped up at the same time. It's almost six AM now. Pretty soon. After I'm done here I'll just go home and crash, because I am dog-assed tired. Then I'll have my date with Carla tonight and life will move forward.

Whether I want it to or not.

And I do want it to move forward. I really do. This in-between shit is wearing me down. I need this trial to be over. I need this bullshit to be put behind me. I need to be able to look myself in the face again.

The door to the garage opens and I sigh.

Finally. The guy takes his goddamned time getting ready. He fumbles with his remote key and doesn't even notice when the alarm doesn't chirp. He's got his arms full of folders and crap and he sets all that down on the roof as he pulls the door open. The dome light stays off, but he's too preoccupied with his phone to notice that either.

Man, this guy is dumb.

He shoves his shit over on the seat next to him, then closes the door and starts the car. It's not until he presses the button on the garage door opener that he finally figures out something is wrong.

I point the gun at his head and say, "Bang, motherfucker. You're dead."

He stiffens and takes in a sharp breath, but he keeps his mouth shut, and that's the first smart thing he's done since I saw him yesterday.

"You know why I'm here, Carson Reed?"

He eyes me in the rear-view and nods.

"Why?"

"Uh…" He clears his throat and tries again. "You're Veronica's… friend. You own that bike shop."

"Well, you got the who down, but I asked you if you know the why."

He swallows hard. "You love her?"

"I do love her. That's exactly why I'm here. What time were you gonna call her and tell her no?"

He squints his eyes at me. "What?"

"Time, motherfucker. What time were you gonna call her today and tell her no?"

"How do you know I was going to call her?"

"Carson, do not fuck with me, OK? What time?"

He stares at me, and maybe it's possible he doesn't know what I'm talking about, but somehow I doubt it. "Four."

"Right before closing? That's a dick move."

"Mr. Shrike, I'm not sure what you think is going on with her and I—"

"She wants a loan, right? To start a business? I'm not sure what, but something that is not tattoos."

"Uh, yeah." He shakes his head. "Then why are you here? I thought you wanted to kill me for finding us together at dinner."

I laugh. "Oh, I do. Believe me. I do. But I need you and there's that little matter of murder being illegal. So no, I'm not going to kill you. I need you."

"For what?" he asks, his voice cracking a little.

"How much money did she ask for?"

"Twenty, why?"

"Twenty grand? And you were gonna tell her *no*?" Fuck, twenty grand. I have that stuffed in my fucking sock drawer at home. I sigh. "Well, Carson, you're not gonna make that call at four, OK? You're gonna make that call at nine AM. You're gonna get her on the phone and you're gonna tell her yes. With conditions."

"I can't, Mr. Shrike! She's got no co-signer, she makes less than two thousand dollars a month, and she's got no down—"

"Carson," I interrupt him, using my angry voice. "Shut the fuck up and listen. You will call her, you will tell her yes. But then once she's all happy and screaming with joy, you tell her the conditions. She needs to have a full-time job. She needs to make thirty-seven grand a year. She needs to buy something big to establish her credit, like a car. And she needs to have all that in a week, or your boss will yank the application and make her reapply. You tell her the reapplication process is more grueling. Tell her once she gets turned down, it's a black mark. You tell her she needs to hustle this shit up pronto, you got it, Carson?"

He just stares at me.

"Carson? I asked you a fucking question."

"Uh, yeah. But… *why*?"

"Why?" I laugh. "You got it right the first time, asshole. I love her. I want her to be happy. I can't be with her right now for obvious reasons, but that doesn't mean

I'm gonna let her go. So you're gonna do me one more favor. You're gonna take her out on dates. Nice places, dinners—"

Carson Reed throws his hands up. "No. Absolutely not. I can't do that, Mr. Shrike. She's..." He stops and physically turns all the way around. "She's..."

"What? She's what?"

"Intense, Mr. Shrike."

"Dammit, quit fucking calling me that. It's Spencer."

"Spencer," he says hurriedly. "She's way out of my league. She's not my type. I mean, she's gorgeous and she's got, well, you know what she's got. But I don't like the wild ones, I like the quiet ones. And Veronica Vaughn is always on the verge of exploding, that's how wound up she is. She's the opposite of *calm*, Spencer. Wild isn't even a wild enough term to describe this girl. She's like a loose cannon, she's like fireworks, she's like—"

"A bomb," I say, cutting him off. I smile. I love this characterization of my Bombshell. She's feisty.

"She's not into me, I'll tell you that right now. I'm not into her. We went on one real date awhile back, but I pretty much knew it would never work right away. She just needs a loan and I've been stringing her along because I didn't want to hurt her feelings. And I'll tell you now, my boss will *never* approve her loan. She's risky—"

"I'm the fucking bank, Reed. God, you are dumb for being so fucking smart. I'm giving her the money, asshole. Just do as I tell you and I'll have that dough deposited into her account in thirty days. It'll look like it came from your bank. All you have to do is make the call today, tell her the conditions, and take her out somewhere fancy and treat her nice, once a week."

"What if she won't go out with me?"

"Make her go, Reed. You tell her you're just friends if you want, but you will take her out and treat her nice once a fucking week."

He squints his eyes at me and then turns so he's facing forward again. "Well, what do I get out of it? You're obviously not going to kill me, so what's my motivation?"

So he does have a spine. That's good to know. "What do you want?"

He smiles in the rear-view, like a kid grinning ear to ear. "A custom bike."

I laugh. "A custom bike? From me? That's like a hundred grand, Reed."

"Wellllll," he says, drawing the words out slowly. "She's worth it, right?"

Damn. The pencil-pusher's got me.

"I want one of those bikes you make and I want to have a say in what it looks like. I think that's fair."

I shrug. What do I care. He's doing me a business favor, I can do him one back. "OK, stop by my house shop tonight and we'll work out the details. But Carson, I need her to understand she must have a job, OK? I offered her a job working for me as my personal assistant a few hours ago. I need her to call me *today* and give me a yes. Push that. Get her to make the call and accept my offer, without letting her know you know about it, and we're on. I'll make you any bike you want."

He turns around in his seat again and we shake on it. "Deal."

CHAPTER ELEVEN

It's six o'clock by the time she makes the call. "Spencer?" she asks after my cheerful, "Yello."

"I thought you hated me, Bombshell? You love me again?"

She sighs and I beam a smile over at Carson. He thumbs me up as he peruses the catalog of accessories for his fucking custom bike.

"Spencer, I've been thinking about your offer. It was very generous. And—" I can actually hear her swallow, that's how loud it is. She's having trouble eating her crow, but I let her stew. She needs to eat the whole bird tonight. Feathers and all. Because she's just not seeing the big picture and I need to her pay attention to what the fuck I'm trying to accomplish here. "I'd like to take you up on that job offer. If it's still available," she adds quickly.

"Well, I was gonna offer it to Carla, the burrito girl at Big City, but I haven't talked to her yet. I don't pick her up for our weekly date until eight."

I can almost feel Ronnie's seething anger over the phone. I look over at Carson and he's shaking his head at me. I put up a hand and wink.

"Well, I want the job. So is it available or not?"

She's mad now and I smile. I like my Bombshell on the verge of exploding. That's the only way I know she's OK. When she's quiet and contemplative, that's when I know she's having trouble. Ronnie is tough as nails, and while *I* understand she really wants to be treated tenderly, she's just not there yet. So the bad-girl routine is all she's got.

"Veronica," I say softly so I can set her back a little.

"Yes?"

"Even if I did offer Carla that job, I'd never choose her over you, baby. Never."

She snorts. "That's funny. You have a date with her tonight though, right?"

"Yes, that's right."

"So if I ask you to take me out instead of her, would you?"

"No, baby. I can't."

"But I can have a job?"

"Yes. The job is yours."

"That makes no sense, Spencer Shrike."

"That's because you have no details, Veronica Vaughn."

"Enlighten me."

"Someday, Bomb. Someday I'll tell you everything. From start to finish. But not tonight." She's silent after that. She might even be crying. "It's a virtual job, remember?"

"Yes," she squeaks out.

"I'll text you all the info to access my email accounts on Monday. We'll start there for now. We don't need to see each other, just texts and phone calls. Got it?"

She's silent for almost ten seconds before she manages to acknowledge me. "Got it, Spencer. I'll talk to you Monday then."

"Right. Oh, and Ronnie?"

"Yeah?" she comes back with some hope in her voice.

"I think you should date that banker. If he's still interested, that is. Because I had Ford check him out, and he's a good guy. I'd like for you to find yourself a good guy, Ronnie. So if I've screwed anything up, I'm sorry. Maybe try and explain I'm just a dick and you're done with me."

This time when she answers I know she's crying. She manages an, "OK," and then the phone beeps three times and the call is over.

"Shit, Shrike," Carson says from his perch on my crappy desk. "That was fucked up."

"She'll get over it, Reed. Just do your part and I'll do mine. You got an idea what you want? Because I really do have to meet Carla soon."

Carson shakes his head at me. "What the hell? Why are you seeing other girls if you love the Bombshell?"

I sigh. "Carla and I go line-dancing on Thursday nights. Ronnie loves to line-dance but I've never gone with her because I just can't afford to be seen with her in public like that. But soon, I *will* be dating her, Carson. Soon. So I'm getting ready for that day. Carla offered to teach me and every Thursday night we practice at the Sundance Saloon. Fridays, I hang out with Renee from the Cat Call. I watch the strippers so people think I'm available. And Renee is the bartender. She flirts with me and I keep an extra eye out for her when the bar gets crazy. They have shit bouncers over there. Saturdays I hang out with Kim from the Broomfield Harley store. She's on a bowling league down there. Ronnie's brothers have a bowling league up here in FoCo. And as soon as life settles down, I'm in. I want to insert myself into Ronnie's life. I want to be accepted by her family and I figure bowling with them is a good way to do that."

Carson laughs a little. "So you're not fucking any other girls?"

"Hell the fuck no. I haven't had a bit of fucking fun since New Year's when I saw Ronnie last. This trial shit, Carson—this trial shit is big fucking time. These people are not playing around. My friends and I are in deep, man. I do not have time to fuck, or drink, or worry about shit like that. Hell, I barely have time to think about the show."

"You really do love her?" He looks at me hard now. Like he's changing his opinion of me on the spot.

"I really do. But by the time I get my chance to tell her, she might not love me back."

"Well, fuck. I really had no clue."

"That's how it has to stay, Reed. You got it? No one can know I love her. No one. Did you see what happened to Rook Corvus last fall?"

Carson nods his head. "Yeah, I felt sorry for her."

"Well, my Ronnie will not survive that. OK? She won't. I cannot have those filthy reporters following her around like animals, trying to ruin her life and make her freak out for the cameras. Rook has no ties to anyone but us. She was easy to protect. Ronnie has all kinds of family. There are so many ways to get to her. So many people she loves who can be hurt to get even. I need to keep her and her entire family safe."

He nods at me. "OK, then. I get it. I'm in."

"In?"

"Yeah, I'm in. I'll keep your secret for you, Shrike. I'm in. I don't know the whole story and frankly, I do not care. But what you guys did last fall… that was some brave shit. Those assholes all need to go to jail. So if keeping my eye on Ronnie helps you finish them off, you can count on me."

I let out a long breath.

I am one lucky motherfucker.

Not because I got away with murder.

Not because I have a TV show.

Not because I came from a good family or was well-educated, or because I can build bikes or paint naked girls.

I'm a lucky guy because I have friends.

And I'm gonna need every single one of them, because the shit is about to get ugly.

End Of Book Shit

WELCOME to the End of Book Shit. I'm kinda cheating on this new EOBS because I actually wrote this in 2015 right before 321 released. But it was such a cool afterthought about the series, and it was on my book blog, not even my JA Huss blog, so practically no one saw it.

So I'm resurrecting it for your pleasure today!

Spencer is in every single book in the Rook & Ronin series. He comes in late in Tragic, but boy does he make an impression. He scoops Rook up when she needs a friend, and just when you start to think this might turn into a triangle, Spencer Shrike does a 180. He's not what he appears to be. But then again, that was the whole point of the series.

Sometimes when I'm writing a later book in a series I recall a little detail in an earlier book that changes everything about the story. This happened with Spencer and Veronica in Bomb. That novella is supposed to be the first book about Spencer, but instead it introduced Veronica the Bombshell Bomb—Spencer's long-time love-interest who has been dumped.

95

In Bomb I start from the beginning and take you back in time to the day Spencer first saw Veronica on their college campus. He proceeds to woo her, and they end up back in his garage where he reveals his customs bikes. Well, he's only got one custom bike at that point in his life.

That bike he shows Ronnie sort of existed in Tragic, but only as a casual detail. Spencer takes Rook to his bike shop where he has lots of custom bikes. This is his future. He's Big Time now. He's got a showroom filled with motorcycles he needs photographed. He wants something from Rook, and he's willing to offer up something big to get her on his side. So he offers her a custom motorcycle.

Rook picks a Shrike Bike resembling a classic Triumph motorcycle that is just sitting in Spencer's shop, so that's the bike he pretties up for her and presents to her in Manic. The bike ends up being called the Shrike Rook. But it used to be something else before Rook claimed it...

I'm pretty sure no one ever thought about that bike again except me. Because when I had to go back to the time when Spencer was first dating Veronica, Spencer was in Veronica's family tattoo shop asking her to give him ink. He drew the tat he wanted and it caught Veronica by surprise. Spencer was surprised too.

The Shrike Rook appears in Tragic, Manic, Panic, Slack, Bomb, and Guns. If I had really planned it better, it would've been in Taut as well. :) But I didn't plan that bike at all. I pulled that classic Triumph design out of my memory for its first appearance in Tragic. I knew a guy once... he had one. But I had no idea Triumph made a model called the Blackbird when I decided to name Rook after a black bird. I had no idea that the Shrike Rook was modeled after the Triumph Blackbird when I put that random memory into Tragic. And the way the whole thing came full circle didn't even hit me until I was writing Bomb and I realized what I had set up by accident.

I think that's the best thing about writing a series like this. Moments when all the little back story details add up to something BIG just because you're making it all up, and most of what you make up is based off things you already know.

The motorcycle means a lot to Rook. It's her one true possession in Panic—something she takes with her on her final quest to put her past behind her. It means a lot to Bomb as well. She has her first Spencer experience on the half built model and she wants it back in Guns. And to Spencer, because it was the first bike he ever built—it was a symbol of his future, what he was capable of.

I resurrected that bike when I wrote Mr. & Mrs. I didn't plan it then either. I had Oliver and Kat up in Five's motorcycle garage, and Oliver was looking for some sexy times on a bike in true Shrike fashion, and Kat points to a dirty old thing propped up in the corner. And when she wipes the dirt off the tank and they see what it is… well, that's when I saw what it was too.

I swear to God, I just stopped and thought about that for a second. How that bike came back over and over again. How it turned into much more than a bike for so many characters.

And there it was, out in a garage in the middle of the Caribbean just waiting for me to find it.

I think it's the little things like this that makes the story come alive, and even though I didn't really plan it out that way, sometimes it's better to create by accident.

I think that might be the quote they put on my gravestone.

"She created stuff by accident."

I'm OK with that.

Book seven in this series is called Guns and is the complete ending of the story arc of Rook, Ronin, Ford, Spencer, and Veronica. And a few new characters too—Ashleigh, Sasha, James, and Merc. All of whom intersect in the book called The Company and standalones called Meet Me In The Dark and Wasted Lust.

So if you're looking to enter a WORLD. If you're looking to meet characters so real, you feel like you know them. If you're looking to go on the ride of your life with Rook and her friends, keep reading, bitches.

I got you.

Thank you for reading, thank you for reviewing, and I'll see you again in the new EOBS of Guns.

Julie
JA Huss

About The Author

JA Huss never wanted to be a writer and she still dreams of that elusive career as an astronaut. She originally went to school to become an equine veterinarian but soon figured out they keep horrible hours and decided to go to grad school instead. That Ph.D wasn't all it was cracked up to be (and she really sucked at the whole scientist thing), so she dropped out and got a M.S. in forensic toxicology just to get the whole thing over with as soon as possible.

After graduation she got a job with the state of Colorado as their one and only hog farm inspector and spent her days wandering the Eastern Plains shooting the shit with farmers.

After a few years of that, she got bored. And since she was a homeschool mom and actually does love science, she decided to write science textbooks and make online classes for other homeschool moms.

She wrote more than two hundred of those workbooks and was the number one publisher at the online homeschool store many times, but eventually she covered every science topic she could think of and ran out of shit to say.

So in 2012 she decided to write fiction instead. That

year she released her first three books and started a career that would make her a New York Times bestseller and land her on the USA Today Bestseller's List eighteen times in the next three years.

Her books have sold millions of copies all over the world, the audio version of her semi-autobiographical book, Eighteen, was nominated for an Audie award in 2016, her book Mr. Perfect was nominated for a Voice Arts Award in 2017 and her book Taking Turns was nominated for an Audie award in 2018.

She also writes book and screenplays with her friend, actor and writer, Johnathan McClain. Their first book, Sin With Me, will release on March 6, 2018. And they are currently working with MGM as producing partners to turn their adaption of her series, The Company, into a TV series.

She lives on a ranch in Central Colorado with her family, two donkeys, four dogs, three birds, and two cats.

If you'd like to learn more about JA Huss or get a look at her schedule of upcoming appearances, visit her website at www.JAHuss.com or www.HussMcClain.com to keep updated on her projects with Johnathan. You can also join her fan group, Shrike Bikes, on Facebook, www.facebook.com/groups/shrikebikes and follow her Twitter handle, @jahuss.

BOMB

www.ingramcontent.com/pod-product-compliance
Lightning Source LLC
Chambersburg PA
CBHW030457130626
46549CB00007B/2760

9 781944 475505